Confederate Battle Stories

Edited by

Martin H. Greenberg
Frank D. McSherry, Jr.
and Charles G. Waugh

August House Publishers
LITTLE ROCK

Printed in the United States of America

10 9 8 7 6 5 4 3 2

LIBRARY OF CONGRESS CATALOGING-IN-PUBLICATION DATA
Confederate battle stories / edited by Martin H. Greenberg,
Frank D. McSherry, Jr., and Charles G. Waugh.— 1st ed.
p.   cm.
Contents: The disbandment of the Army of Northern Virginia / Marshall
Thompson — Jack Still / J.P. Marquand — A debt of honor / F. Scott
Fitzgerald — O captain! my captain! / H. Bedford-Jones — Gettysburg / Mary
Johnston — Chickamauga / Thomas Wolfe — The rebel trace / Joseph
Hergesheimer — The bloodhounds / W.C. Morrow — Affair at St. Albans /
Herbert Ravenel Sass — The second Missouri compromise / Owen Wister —
The centennial comment / Robert Edmond Alter.
ISBN 0-87483-192-X (hb: alk. paper) : $18.95
ISBN 0-87483-191-1 (pbk: alk. paper) : $9.95
1. United States—History—Civil War, 1861–1865—Fiction.2. Confederate
States of America—History—Fiction. 3. War stories, American—Southern
States. 4. Southern States—Fiction.
[1. United States—History—Civil War, 1861–1865—Fiction. 2. Short stories.]
I. Greenberg, Martin Harry. II. McSherry, Frank D. III. Waugh, Charles G.
PS648.C54C66   1992
813′.0108358—dc20   91-44892

First edition, 1992

Executive: Liz Parkhurst
Project Editor: Judith Faust
Editorial assistant: Susan Moore
Cover design and illustration: Wendell E. Hall
Typography: Lettergraphics/Little Rock

This book is printed on archival-quality paper which meets
the guidelines for performance and durability of the
Committee on Production Guidelines for Book Longevity of the
Council on Library Resources.

AUGUST HOUSE, INC.   PUBLISHERS   LITTLE ROCK

Acknowledgments

"Jack Still," by J.P. Marquand, is reprinted by permission of Fiduciary Trust Company for the C.M. Welch Trust.

"O Captain! My Captain!," copyright 1943 by H. Bedford–Jones, is reprinted by permission of the agents for the author's estate, Scott Meredith Literary Agency, Inc., 845 Third Avenue, New York, New York 10022.

"Chickamauga," by Thomas Wolfe, is taken from *The Hills Beyond* (copyright 1939 by Maxwell Perkins). It is reprinted by permission of the Estate of Thomas Wolfe.

"The Rebel Trace," by Joseph Hergesheimer, first appeared in the *Saturday Evening Post* and is reprinted by permission of the Estates of Joseph Hergesheimer and Dorothy Hergesheimer.

"Affair at St. Albans," by Herbert Ravenel Sass, first appeared in the *Saturday Evening Post* in March 1948 (copyright renewed 1976 by the Estate of Herbert Ravenel Sass). It is reprinted by permission of the Estate of Herbert Ravenel Sass.

"The Second Missouri Compromise," by Robert Edmond Alter, first appeared in *Adam* magazine in February 1968 (copyright 1968 by Knight Publishing Corp.). It is reprinted by permission of the Larry Sternig Literary Agency.

Contents

Always Outnumbered—
Never Outfought

Southrons, hear your country call you...
To arms! To arms! To arms in Dixie!
See the beacon fires are lighted!
—Albert Pike, General, CSA

As snow fell in an artificial moonlight made by searchlight beams pointing up to a layer of dark clouds, thousands of Panzer tanks clanked and crunched forward on Christmas Eve to strike at the junction of the British and American armies in France, in a last, bloody effort by the Nazis to punch through our lines, to drive to the sea, to create another Dunkirk—a drive that almost succeeded.

Tough opponents?

Hell, no.

Not compared to the warriors of the Confederacy and some of the generals who led them, men justly ranked by historians as military geniuses: courtly Robert E. Lee, an iron hand in a velvet glove; hard-driving, black-bearded "Old Pete" Longstreet; hot-eyed "Stonewall" Jackson, grim as an Old Testament prophet; and the romantic cavalryman, "Jeb" Stuart.

The infantry tended to be young, unsophisticated, poorly educated, dressed in faded homespun with rope-tied blanket rolls on their backs, short of muskets, food, and shoes. In 1862, at Second Manassas, witnesses told of seeing Confederate soldiers eating salt by the handful at a captured Union supply depot. A wounded Union officer at Fredericksburg woke on the battlefield to find his new boots being removed by a Confederate private, who turned red and said, "I beg yore pardon, sir; I thought you had passed away."

These were the men who made the famous, heart-stopping charge at Gettysburg, who fought to the last bloody inch.

The Civil War was "the costliest, most deadly war America ever fought," said historian Bruce Catton. "More than 500,000 soldiers lost their lives, in a country whose entire population, North and South together, numbered hardly more than 30 million. If battle losses in World War II had been in proportion, we would have had 2,500,000 men killed—exclusive of those wounded and missing." And this with muskets whose maximum rate of fire was two rounds a minute!

What makes this all the more remarkable is that the Confederate soldier was almost always outnumbered. Against a Union population of nineteen million, the South had only twelve million people, and a third of those were slaves whom the Southern leadership refused to draft.

The bare feet of Confederate soldiers, comfortable on the dirt roads of the South, left a literal trail of blood on the macadam roads of the North, "limping along so painfully," said a lady who saw them on Lee's first invasion of the North, "trying to keep up with their comrades."

Their valor was unsurpassed, their devotion undying—if worthy of a better cause.

The stories included here were chosen because they're good stories, yet they are more than mere entertainment. They portray the characteristics of the Confederate soldier at all levels of command. They tell us not only about the Southern soldier, but about the society that created him and why, in the long run, he lost.

In J.P. Marquand's novelette "Jack Still," a Confederate officer tells President Jefferson Davis as darkness falls on the battlefield of Bull Run that the Yankees are fleeing in panic and there is nothing standing between the Confederates and the capture of Washington. Give the order to advance, he says, and we will win the war in twenty-four hours! The answer he gets shakes his view of the South's leader and his hopes for Southern success.

The virtues of the Confederate soldier are shown in F. Scott Fitzgerald's account of courage lost and regained in the ranks, while in "Gettysburg," Mary Johnson explores a vice—overconfidence. Lee was warned that no 15,000 men God ever made could take the all-too-well-named Cemetery Ridge, but he launched Pickett's Charge anyway, only to see it shattered in blood and carnage by Union artillery. He had believed the Confederate soldier capable of anything. "I thought he could do it," Lee said.

Yet the spirit lives on.

Former Confederate General Robert Toombs, a fire-eater of the Old South, was asked by a Union friend after the war if he had applied for the pardon offered by the United States government to former Confederates.

"Pardon for what?" Toombs snapped. "I have not pardoned you all yet!"

Turn the page, then...

Here they come. Fifteen thousand strong, the Confederate soldiers of Pickett's Division, the tramp of marching quiet at first but getting louder and louder, moving forward in broad daylight under a hot bright July sky toward the artillery-rimmed heights of Cemetery Ridge, where General Henry Hunt's Union guns wait for them—moving toward red roaring death and the immortality of legend.

Valor unsurpassed.

Frank D. McSherry, Jr.

The Disbandment of the Army of Northern Virginia

MARSHALL THOMPSON

We rode past the curve, and saw in the gathering twilight the yellow Virginia road winding ahead for miles, nothing else to break the monotony of the ranks of pines except a weather-beaten shanty that stood lonely among the trees. In front, a rude flag-pole sentineled the way; and at the peak fluttered in the evening breeze, thirty years after the war had ended, the tattered and faded, but still to be distinguished, red field, divided by the blue St. Andrew's Cross, of the last battle-flag of the Southern Confederacy.

As the sun slowly sank behind the pines, the notes of a bugle sounded among the trees. Then a rifle shot rang from the cabin, and an old man, erect as a soldier, walked, or rather marched, to the flag-pole, and gently lowered the flag. As it fluttered to the ground, I noticed that the Virginia colonel with whom I rode had uncovered and that a look of other days had come into his face.

"What does it mean?" I asked.

"It is the last headquarters of the Army of Northern Virginia," he laughed in reply.

Afterwards I heard the story, partly from the Colonel, partly from others.

When the War broke out and the strains of "Dixie," from the Gulf to Baltimore, were setting bright eyes and brave hearts a-dancing, Company F was being recruited in Albemarle County, Virginia. The privates were gentlemen's sons from neighboring plantations; the officers, wealthy land-owners of the vicinity; the equipment of the best, the uniforms being of fine gray cloth and made in London; and Company F was considered—at least in Albemarle County— "the finest company of the finest State in or out of the Union, sah."

In the community of Ivy Church there was only one man of military age not in Company F. He was an Irishman, Patrick Murphy, once a sergeant in the British army, now a "land-owner and a gintleman." He had an acre or two in the country. He raised vegetables, and sold them when he could, smoked his pipe, and was happy. Patrick had not been asked to join the company when it was organized, for the young cavaliers had no desire for the society of a man who worked with his hands and was, in their opinion, "little better than a nigger."

As the days of drilling wore away, all was not sunshine in Company F. The officers, with the best intentions in the world, knew absolutely nothing of drill and military discipline, and of course the men could not be blamed for ignorance when there was no adequate instruction. Meanwhile, Patrick Murphy stood an on-looker and watched with amused contempt the movements of "th' recruities."

When Captain De Courcy (ex-West-Pointer) took charge of the company, things rapidly changed for the better; but it took all the company's enthusiasm and all its respect for De Courcy to keep from open protest when the captain announced that Patrick Murphy must and should be enlisted.

"He is an ex-sergeant," said De Courcy; "has served in the British army; and we've got to have a good non-commissioned officer or we'll go all to pieces at the first fire; the men marched this afternoon like a lot of brats with broomsticks."

"But a common Irishman to be placed over gentlemen!"

"And mighty lucky for the gentlemen," said De Courcy. "You gentlemen must learn that there are just two classes in the army—officers and privates. Other things being equal, I should prefer to have gentlemen privates; but I have had Irishmen, Englishmen, Germans, and niggers, and they all come out about the same under a good sergeant."

"Not niggers!"

"Yes, niggers. They're all right when properly drilled, and you fellows will admit it too before this war is over," and with this heretical remark De Courcy went to his quarters.

So Patrick Murphy was enlisted. He knew something of the feeling in the company, and when he had signed the papers and taken the oath of allegiance to the sovereign State of Virginia, he turned to the on-lookers and said:

"I'm the lasht man of this coompany to enlisht; but tak' notice, I'll be th' lasht wan to dishband."

The influence of Murphy as drill-master was immediately apparent: the lines straightened out, the men became erect, the company wheeled like clockwork, and the manual of arms went with the click and precision of machinery. Then came the day when they marched off—

> *"Away down South in Dixie,*
> *Look away, look away."*

How well the old Virginians remember it! The line in front of the court-house steps; the girls in their big bonnets and voluminous skirts; the fathers and mothers and sweethearts; the cheer, the sob, and the laugh! The presentation of the flag—"the blue flag of Virginia—blue as the sky, woven by the fair hands of the ladies of Albemarle County—given to the sons of heroic sires, the best blood of the Old Dominion—gentlemen." "May it wave in victory!" "May it never know defeat!" "Hurrah!—three cheers for the ladies of Albemarle County!" "Good-by! Good-by!"

> *"Away down South in Dixie,*
> *Look away, —look—"*

The line has passed down the street, out on the yellow road, and the pine trees hide it.

More than thirty years ago, ladies and gentlemen of Virginia; but the days of '61 still live in the hearts of your faded women and white-haired men who entertain us, the sons of the Northern invaders of other days, with your generous hospitality; still live in your hearts, with no thought of bitterness or disloyalty; but they were your boys, and they lie from Bull Run to Appomattox—but to you, still young, still confident, ever marching on in the spring sunshine, the bonny blue flag waving over them—

"Away down South in Dixie,
Look away, look away."

Patrick Murphy marched away with the company; in the first engagement saved the flag, and became color-sergeant; went to West Virginia and back to Manassas; fought at Fair Oaks and Seven Pines; tramped on the wonderful night march through the Shenandoah valley; kept time to the

"Maryland, my Maryland"

of the bands, as regiment after regiment crossed the river in the shadow of the hills, and swung over the dusty road on the march to Frederick. After Antietam, was offered and refused a commission; stood in the line of flame and death at Fredericksburg and Chancellorsville; marched with the tattered and ragged, but till now victorious, army of Northern Virginia on the second invasion of the North; retreated, as lighthearted in defeat as in victory, from Gettysburg, and after each reverse of the Wilderness laughed and said, "We'll lick 'em worse nixt toime."

The next times grew sad for the army of Northern Virginia. Day by day came news of fresh losses, fresh defeats on the Gulf, in the West. Rumors of Sherman's march thickened, while in front their old enemy, the Army of the Potomac, ever persistent, with a commander at last who understood his trade, pressed relentlessly forward. At last came the feeling that the very stars in their courses fought for the Northern battalions—Petersburg, Cold Harbor—and the army, starving, ragged, but gallant still, was for the first time in its history in real retreat. Here and there a man slipped away in the night, sure that the war was practically over; now a company lost ten and a regiment a hundred; but the majority, ragged, shoeless, shirtless, munched their parched corn, marched on, fought on, to Appomattox; and with the majority marched and fought Patrick Murphy.

As General Lee, "flower of Southern chivalry" indeed, rode back from his interview with Grant, his escort, respecting his feelings, fell back, while the General, with head bowed, let his horse choose his own way back to the defeated army. Suddenly his revery was disturbed; a thin, sunburned sergeant, carrying a flag, stepped from the bushes, halted, and came to attention.

"Gineral Lee."

"Yes, my man."

"Me name is Patrick Murphy."

"Well?"

"Gineral Lee, the bys say that the Arrmy of Northern Virginia is surrindered and will dishband."

"Yes, my man. The army is to give its parole never to bear arms against the United States, turn in its arms and accoutrements, but keep its horses, and disband."

Patrick Murphy shifted uneasily from foot to foot, while the General watched him curiously, doubtless glad that the train of his gloomy thoughts should be broken by the interruption. Suddenly a twinkle came into Murphy's eyes.

"Gineral Lee, if wan division of th' Arrmy of Northern Virginia should refuse to dishband, that wad still be the Arrmy of Northern Virginia, wouldn't it, Gineral Lee?"

"Yes, my man."

"If two rigiments or a brigade should refuse to dishband, that wad be the Arrmy, wouldn't it?"

"Yes, my man," replied the General, wondering what the whimsical Celtic brain was evolving.

"Gineral Lee, if all th' officers an' all th' soldiers of the Arrmy of Northern Virginia except wan company should dishband, that company wad be the Arrmy of Northern Virginia?"

"Yes, yes, my man." The General was getting impatient, and lifted his bridle rein.

"Wan minute more—if th' Gineral plaze, sor! If all that wan coompany should dishband except wan man, that man wad be the Arrmy, sor, wouldn't he, Gineral Lee?"

The General's eyes twinkled at the conceit, but answered gravely as before, "Yes, my man, I suppose he would."

Murphy stood even more erect than before. "Gineral Lee, I refuse to dishband." Then turning half front, his voice ringing with the tone of command, "Arrmy of Northern Virginia, about face! Forward march! Report at Ivy Church, Virginia!" and off he marched whistling, not "Dixie," but the "Wearing of the Green."

When Colonel Marshall, who was on escort duty, rode up, he wondered as he heard for the first time in many weary months a hearty laugh ring from the General's lips.

General Lee forgot the matter entirely; but when the Army of Northern Virginia gave in its parole, one name was missing—that of Patrick Murphy—and one battle-flag was never accounted for; it was the one I had seen fluttering down from the staff among the pine trees thirty years after the war ended, where Patrick Murphy, in sunshine and shadow, held his cabin, the last stronghold of the dead Confederacy, against his one enemy—old age, and maintained under the branches of the pines the organization of the Army of Northern Virginia.

Here I supposed the story of the disbandment of the Army of Northern Virginia would end; but in May of this year I again rode down through the pines, and again the Colonel rode with me. This time he rode in a blue uniform, and the letters U.S.V. glittered on the collar. In front marched, as in '61, the young men of Ivy Church; but their uniforms were blue, and the national flag kissed the sunlight above the marching ranks. There had been the scenes of 1861 reënacted before the court-house steps, and a new picture of marching men and a proudly tossing flag had been painted, never to fade by the years, and again the old Confederate tune set the eyes and the hearts a-dancing:

> *"Away down South in Dixie,*
> *Look away, look away."*

Patrick Murphy came from his cabin, and saluted the Colonel. He was dressed in the tattered gray of Company F, in his hands the furled battle-flag.

"I want th' officer commanding this coompany."

"I am he," said the Colonel.

"Captain—for that's your rank now—the Arrmy of Northern Virginia"—a twinkle danced in the faded blue eyes—"the Arrmy of Northern Virginia wants to enlist as an organization, to fight"—his eyes lost their twinkle, and his face took on a new look of dignity—"for the United States."

The Colonel waited a moment. "You are too old," he said.

"Then it's toime to tak' th' oath of allegiance and dishband," said Murphy. "There is wan flag for us now, and it's not this," and he held up the old flag.

Fresh and clear came the music of the band:

"Away down South in Dixie,
Look away, look away."

As the flag passed—his flag at last—the old man uncovered and stood at salute.

"In Dixie's land I take my stand,
To live and die for Dixie."

The Colonel was silent. Wilder and more rollicking came the music, the dust rolled up in a cloud, and still Patrick Murphy stood at attention.

"By Jove, the war is over!" exclaimed the Colonel. "Order them to play the 'Star Spangled Banner.'"

Jack Still

J.P. Marquand

Scott Mattaye liked to tell the story best in the library at Deer Bottom Plantation, of how he saw a slender, thin-nosed man hold the destiny of a nation in his hand one July night some sixty years before.

You could believe anything he had seen when he told of it in the library, because the uncouth, varied shadows of the Confederacy had never left it. There was a memory of crinoline and long-tailed coats, the memory of an era prodigious in its extremes, and the room had the marks of war.

The cold steel engravings on the wall represented landscapes as peaceful as the views on Worcester ware. He could understand why the memory of those pictures had come to him at the very instant that a polite and self-effacing civilian had presented a pocket pistol at his heart in the woods beyond Bull Run. The books were on their cracked, varnished shelves in almost the same order they had stood before the war, as old as Scott Mattaye and as wholly out of place.

"Sammy," he would say to the cook's small son, "yo' shif'less boy, raise yore candle so the gentlemen can see."

The titles on the crumbling calfskin bindings were half obliterated by dust and mold. There were forgotten works of Southern genius, unknown above the Line, surrounded by the pungent smell of decaying leather. It always seemed to Scott Mattaye that they represented what might have been, now grown as dry and sterile as the dust; he never could avoid bitterness, once he saw the books. He could feel the grip of invasion again, blundering and inexorable; and it still held his house, for the cavalry had stopped there once. The Yankee power was in that library, an uncouth alien force, stamping out the leisured cultivation of a landed gentry.

"Sammy," he would say, "hold up yore candle!... Yonder—there's where they cut out the paintings. You see the frames?"

Three gilt frames, just above the books, surrounded nothing but a shadowy blankness. Although they had hung barren for sixty years against the peeling wallpaper, the sight of them was still startling. The smug intellectual snobbery of the place was no longer amusing, once you saw the frames, and the silence seemed to leave it.

Scott Mattaye was the one who could see it leave. When the candle flickered, the light came back, distorted, from the black windows like a flame. It was like the sweep of fire outside, when the corncribs and the barns and smokehouse had been burning. The horses on the lawn beneath the tulip trees would be pulling at their bridles. The house was full of footsteps and of nasal, ugly voices....They must have been a detachment from Cooke's or Pleasonton's. They would be gawky dry-goods or ribbon clerks, who could not ride.

"Sammy," he would say, "set down that candle and fetch refreshment for the gentlemen....I know what I'm saying. No Yankee cavalry would have got here, gentlemen, because at the first Bull Run we might have won the war. We had 'em whipped, I'm saying. We'd have picketed in the Washington City Capitol. I know and I believe, for I was there. I heard 'em talking."

He had heard and, once his memory started working, he could bring it back. He was young, in Stuart's cavalry again, and he had seen a nation hanging in the balance in the second-floor room of a rickety frame house the night after Bull Run was fought, and it had been as prosaic as the plantation library.

The candle guttered on the table. The empty frames were staring down, framing Scott Mattaye's belief, and his voice was shaken with it.

"It wasn't a retreat. It was a rout," he was saying. "The only time there was a rout. We had only to go."

The strength of his conviction echoed like Walt Whitman's words in a distant, mysterious cadence which was growing louder as he spoke: "...all the men with this coating of muck and sweat and rain, now recoiling back, pouring over the Long Bridge....They drop down any-where—on the steps of the houses, up close to the basements or fences, on the sidewalks, aside on some vacant lot....Some in squads; comrades, brothers, close together—and on them, as they lay, sulkily drips the rain."

Longstreet was arguing with an officer from Johnston's staff; Federal teamsters were cutting traces at Cub Run; panic was sweeping over an improvised Union army and dark was falling. Jackson was calling for ten thousand men....

"Yes, sir," Scott Mattaye was saying, "I heard them talking in the room. The door was open, and I was standing there. They didn't see me, and I heard them. I couldn't think what else to do....He was a thin man in a black frock coat, thin nosed, handsome, like his statue, and it's what I say. We might have won that war. He held it in his hand like this—right there in his hand."

Human frailty and vanity and the irony of little things, working in an integration that made destiny—Scott Mattaye had seen it all. He had seen the destiny of gambler's luck that holds the balance of a war. And it started with a gambler—it was as strange as that—a fantastic figure who had leveled a pocket pistol at his heart.

He was asleep at Sudley Springs, Scott always said, where Stuart's cavalry had halted after following the retreat, and sleep in war was different from other sleep. Even when Scott Mattaye started from the depths—and he could be conscious in a moment—the curtain of sleep would be so close behind him that reality was blurred, mercifully, into the elements of dreaming. That was why the beginning was always like a dream; he was sleeping on the ground when someone gripped his shoulder.

"You, Mattaye." Though he was only half awake, he knew the voice. It was Colonel Stuart speaking, and Scott Mattaye could have sworn the colonel never slept. "Get up, Mattaye."

First he thought that they were in the woods on Henry House Hill, and that he would hear the guns, but there was no sound of firing. Then he felt the hardness of the ground and the damp. There was a smell of horses and leather, and the dank smells of late evening. He was on the ground outside headquarters near the ford.

"You hear me?" the colonel said. "I want you to carry a message. Come inside."

The colonel had taken over the kitchen of a small log house. The room was typically a poor man's; Scott Mattaye could even remember the smell of milk pails, kerosene and bacon fat; and though half awake, he could see unfinished timbers, an open hearth and crane, a rough-hewn trestle table and handmade chairs. There was a lantern on the table, two pistols and a pen and paper. Two officers with their cloaks around them were sleeping on the floor, and a trooper from the picket was standing near the wall with an inconspicuous man beside him in clothes which were smeared with dust. Scott would never have noticed that man except he was a civilian and a stranger.

"Mattaye," said the colonel, and he took off his slouch hat and laid it on the table; and Scott remembered that his hair was neatly brushed and parted on the side. He was magnificent there in the kitchen, already assuming the stature of the great cavalry leader of the war. It seemed as though the drabness of the place were made to set him off, the perfect background of a picture. J.E.B. Stuart must have felt it, for he had the dramatic sense. His blue eyes glistened; bronze lights were glowing in his beard; he tucked his buckskin gloves into his yellow sash and pulled down his gray shell jacket. He must have known the man by the wall was watching him, and he was never afraid of being watched.

"Mattaye, there's some coffee on the fire—right good coffee....And now, stranger, you step forward, please, and we'll get finished. My name's Stuart—J.E.B. Stuart—late of the United States Army, and now commanding the First Virginia Cavalry of the Confederate States of America, and you were taken by my picket. May I ask your name?"

The man in the dusty clothes moved into the light politely and deliberately. Though he was soiled and bedraggled, he was expensively dressed. There was a diamond on his finger and a red-stone pin in his cravat, and he wore a black-and-green embroidered vest of watered silk. Yet there was nothing vulgar; he was almost like a gentleman. His hair was half long, black and oiled; his face was ageless and impassive.

"Excuse me, suh," he said; "I've stated to you"—his voice was soft and almost toneless, and as undisturbing as a whisper—"previously that I gave myse'f up with the greatest pleasure to yore picket, suh. I had the definite and patriotic purpose of conveyin' my information to yore lines in the interest of a cause which I admire, suh, and which is so ably prosecuted by such an officer as I see before me—no flattery intended. My name is Still—Jack Still—and relieved to be in the company of a discriminatin' gentleman, an' not with them damn Yankees."

He paused and rubbed his hands together—delicate white hands, beautifully precise. The colonel sat down behind the table and tilted backward in his chair, but even in that restful attitude he did not appear relaxed.

"I place you now," he said. "A Mississippi gambler, aren't you, Mr. Still?"

"Yes, suh, to be frank," said Mr. Still. "At gentlemen's service on river steamers, peacetimes. Findin' myself in Washington City, I followed with this Yankee army as far as Centerville, helpin' these officers to divert themselves, suh. Not gentlemen, suh; all of 'em small tradesmen, most graspin' and suspicious. There would have been no misunderstandin' in the game if they could have taken losses like Southern gentlemen."

The voice of that man, Scott always said, was as soothing as a benediction, as placid as his eyes, healing frayed nerves and lulling the mind to rest.

"Chased out, eh?" Colonel Stuart said.

"Yes, suh," said Mr. Still. "Frankly, suh, there was an embarrassin' misunderstandin'. I tell you, suh, there's no such thing as honor in that damn Yankee army."

The colonel was smiling and playing with the knot of his saber.

"Killed a man, eh?" he said.

There was an instant's pause. The stranger closed his eyes and opened them, but there was no expression in his face or voice.

"Colonel," he answered, "I fail to understand."

Yet Scott Mattaye knew as sure as fate that a killer was in the room, and that the very peacefulness of Mr. Still was dangerous.

"Don't argue," the colonel said. "It's a right odd thing that parties like you should help to win a war. You're the only man across this run tonight who's seen the Yankees running, if you tell the truth, but—Suppose I send you back. Speak up; how would you like that?"

Mr. Still sighed, and suddenly his lips curled up in a faint, slow smile.

"I'd prefer the colonel wouldn't, since he asks—always considerin' I've come here with valuable information, suh."

The colonel rose from his chair, and his spurs clinked softly as he walked across the floor. He stood looking straight at Mr. Still, and Mr. Still gazed back, enigmatic and serene.

"All right," he said; "I won't send you back, but I hope very much, mister, you're sure of everything you saw."

"You can count it right, suh," said Mr. Still. "I heard staff officers talking, and I saw the thing myself. I know when a party's busted, suh. There's nothin' between you-all and Washington City that you can call a fightin' force. The Yankee army's busted, suh. It's gone!"

"Mr. Still," the colonel said, "I've taken down your statement, and I'll send you to headquarters. It's the first time in your life you're valuable to anybody, or I miss my guess....Saddle up a horse for the prisoner, Mattaye."

The man's eyes flickered, though his face was impassive.

"Prisoner, colonel?" he said. "Sholy there's no need for that. Why, here I come of my own accord, bringin' information from a Yankee staff. Sholy you don't mean to hold me prisoner and send me to headquarters? Why, colonel, it isn't nohow justice! Respectfully, I'd much prefer simply to be allowed to pass along."

"So that's it, is it?" the colonel said. "You're in trouble this side, too, are you, Mr. Still? Out of the frying pan into the fire—is that the way it is?"

"Now, suh," Mr. Still replied, "I didn't affirm such a thing, but a man like me, he has enemies, colonel. As one gentleman to another—and I come of good stock, suh—I ask leave to go my way, colonel, if you please."

The colonel turned to the table and picked up a letter.

"Mattaye," he said, "carry this and conduct this man to headquarters at Manassas. And you deliver this letter to the commanding general. You understand, Mattaye? This man has been searched, but keep an eye on him and be careful, understand? Shoot him if he tries to break away. Don't stop, don't argue. Shoot him. Still, you hear me? Mattaye, you understand?"

Stuart's eyes were on him, amiable and blue, and he spoke without malice or anger, the way he always spoke:

"Don't be afraid to kill him; you understand, Mattaye?"

Scott Mattaye stood at attention, and he felt the prisoner looking at him carefully.

"Yes, sir," said Scott Mattaye, but beneath the glance of Mr. Still he felt inadequate and young. "Yes, sir; he'll be all right."

Mr. Still straightened the pin in his cravat and smiled his faint, slow smile.

"If you insist, suh," he said. "Good night. We'll have a right nice ride."

Manassas was a good six miles away from Sudley Springs. Scott Mattaye remembered thinking that the distance seemed immense, now that he and his civilian were outside; and he still had the sense of being only half awake as they started down the road. Later, given a year of war, such an incident would have seemed like nothing, but he could not escape the unreality, then, that he should be riding with a man a half length forward to the left, whom he was told to shoot should he try to break away.

Mr. Still did not seem dangerous. His voice was sympathetic, soft and friendly.

"Trooper," he said, "I'm right ashamed to be givin' you such trouble. You must be downright tired after all this fightin'?"

"Yes," said Scott. "You keep a mite forward, please, and don't start dropping back."

"Pardon, suh," said Mr. Still. "It's the hoss. He's tired too. Trooper, let's talk sense. I'm famed for being sensible. It's why I'm livin' now. For instance, I see you fingerin' your weapon—a sight which always sets me shiverin'. Those new pistols are amazing accurate, even when a greenhorn pulls 'em. Excuse me, trooper, no offense. I'm simply demonstratin' that I won't run. I couldn't get off on this horse the colonel's loaned me. And, trooper, I've been searched. There's no more poison in me than a bunny. Will you tell me where you come from, suh?"

"Deer Bottom," said Scott Mattaye. "My people are planters there."

"Are they so?" said Mr. Still. "Of co'se, the Mattayes. I should have recollected—the very finest quality."

Scott Mattaye felt better after that. He only wondered later why Mr. Still should have recollected, or why he should have known.

They had passed the church at Sudley Springs. There were the lanterns of a field hospital beside the road, and teams were creaking past them, moving toward Manassas with the wounded. There was a slow, limping traffic all along that road, punctuated by lantern lights which flashed on sights that were like delirious thoughts—pale faces like souls in purgatory, smashed fences, blankets, haversacks.

"It must have been a mighty battle hereabouts," said Mr. Still. "It's consolin' to be riding with good blood. There's nothing like good blood. Why, trooper, a single Southern gentleman can whip a dozen Yankees. Yes, indeed, I know."

"Yes?" said Scott. "Will you kindly keep up forward, if you please?"

"Pardon," said Mr. Still. "It's just this pesky hoss. Bein' quality, you sholy know the officers at this headquarters staff where we're going. I wonder—there's a certain colonel. He resembles me a mite."

"I'm just a trooper, mister," said Scott. "I don't have truck with officers. I've never seen a one that looks like you."

"None the less," said Mr. Still, "he's yonder. Yes, he's yonder."

The night was sultry and heavy, like any July night at home, except that there was something shocked about the dark, as though a frightful thing had happened and the country where they were riding seemed to be recovering from a blow. They were riding down a rolling slope, where one could see a row of campfires far over to the left, and the dim line of a road, and lights about an old stone house. They were crossing the battlefield in the same direction the troops had moved that morning when they had struck the Southern flank. They were riding toward the pike over an open country. The crests of fields were visible against the sky. He could see the lanterns of details still searching for the wounded, jolting, stopping and moving on; and he could hear voices across the fields above the rattling of the wagons. Except for the fires and the lanterns, there was life only upon the road. Everything was dreaming in the night, and he could feel the dream. Outrageous memories were surrounding him, and he seemed like a ghost revisiting that place.

"Trooper," said Mr. Still, "there must be heaps of dead men here."

"Yes," said Scott, "over all those fields. First they drove us and then they broke."

"A very interestin' sight," said Mr. Still. "And where's Manassas now?"

"About three miles away," said Scott. "This here was our left."

"I understand," said Mr. Still, "you whipped 'em pretty, and why you're not still driving after is more than I can see. I wish I had been with you. I should have been, except a man like me, who's lived like me, has no place much to go."

They were out of the fields, moving through thick oak woods, when Scott Mattaye began to notice that Mr. Still kept looking back. Scott could see the white of his face turn toward him and then away. They rode at a trot past a line of wagons, and the road was clear ahead.

"Friend," said Mr. Still, "may I ride close? I want to talk in a confidential way."

"No," said Scott, "you ride up where you are."

"Very good," said Mr. Still, and he half turned in his saddle. "Then from this position I'm laying my cards on the table for a show-down, friend. They searched me back yonder, but, trooper, I've got five hundred in bills in my right boot, and it's all clear yours if you'll let me ride away. Don't stop me. Listen, friend; I've personal reasons not to go to this headquarters. There's someone there who'll know me. For private reasons, I don't pine for that."

"Why?" asked Scott. "Who's going to hurt you, mister?"

"Five hundred dollars," repeated Mr. Still. "I can pay when my luck is running bad. It's the personal disgrace. Are you listenin', friend?"

"Listen you'se'f," said Scott. "It won't help to talk to me."

"I hope it will," said Mr. Still, "for I'm simply appealing to your kindness. I can't go with you, trooper. I repeat there's a party at headquarters who will know me, and it will be embarrassin' to us both. I'm wanted in Louisiana—wanted bad by law. I came here to tell what I'd seen, but not to be held, and I can't afford to be on exhibition no way. I toss five hundred in the pot, and I ask to be let go."

Scott Mattaye could still remember, and he could feel his own breath catch again, though that man was a stranger to him always, who had come out of nothing to strike and go away. There they were riding down the road, thrown together for an instant like sticks in a whirlpool. He could almost believe that he was still asleep.

"You—what?" said Scott Mattaye.

Mr. Still turned in his saddle, an impassive, slouching shadow, and his voice was very patient:

"I'm speakin' to a gentleman, who would understand if I could explain what circumstances prevent me explainin', suh. I can only repeat, respectfully, five hundred and thanks, if you just will let me go."

Then Scott was angry. "Mister," he said, "you don't know who you're speaking to. Turn around and ride."

He should have known better, though it did not seem possible that he could be troubled on an open, traveled road. His pistol was still in his holster, but the event occurred so suddenly that he could never quite explain. Mr. Still's horse reared, and before Scott could draw a rein they both were close abreast. Then Scott felt something press against his side. Mr. Still was pointing a pocket pistol directly at his heart. The night was dark, but he could see the weapon. There was no doubt; Mr. Still was holding a pistol at his heart.

"Don't," said Mr. Still. "Trooper, don't you move or holler. Turn off yonder, right smack among those trees."

Scott turned. There was no doubting the man's voice, in spite of its softness; he would be dead if he did not turn. Then they were on a wood road in a thicket of scrub oak.

"There," said Mr. Still; "that's right and neat. Keep your hoss still walking. No one's going to hold me where folks I know can stare. Yore colonel thinks he's smart, trooper, but he don't match hands with me. I keep a pocket derringer in my sleeve, and, mind you, she can speak."

Scott did not answer, and Mr. Still's voice rose a note:

"Keep yore hand off that pistol butt, unless you want to die. And get down off your hoss. I'm downright sorry, trooper, but I'm going to take both these hosses and tie you to this tree."

"Suppose," said Scott; his voice was thick—"suppose I don't get down."

Though it was too dark to see, he knew that Mr. Still was smiling.

"I'm much afraid," said Mr. Still, "yo'll naturally fall off. This derringer don't look like much, but don't get passionate. Gentlemen are always so powerful rash....Just swing down off that horse."

He remembered what Jeb Stuart said. Nothing could hurt a cavalryman if he had a good horse under him. He leaned to the left and shifted his weight as though preparing to dismount, at the same time gathering his reins more to the left than right. Then he let drive with his spurs at almost the same instant. Scott's mare sprang, striking Still's horse on the shoulder. There was a crack of a pistol, and Scott's left arm felt red hot, but his right was free, and he fired, in that tangle of two plunging horses, point-blank at Mr. Still.

He remembered how his pistol kicked backward in his hand. An oak branch whipped across his eyes, blinding him for an instant. Mr. Still's horse had bolted, when he saw again, and all that remained was something black on the wood road. Mr. Still was lying face downward, quiet and inert. Scott touched him with his toe, but he might as well have touched a bag of meal.

"Still!" said Scott. "You hear me, Still?"

But Mr. Still did not reply. He simply lay there, a dark spot on the road. There was a candle end in his saddlebag. The air was so still that the candle burned smoothly when Scott lighted it. Mr. Still lay in the sphere of light, elegantly listless. His pistol had dropped and lay six inches beyond the reach of his thin fingers.

"Still!" said Scott again. "You hear me?" But Mr. Still did not reply. Scott set down the candle upon a flat stone, seized Mr. Still by the shoulders and propped him against a tree. Mr. Still's face was blank and incurious; his cravat was twisted and covered with leaf mold. There was a stain on his brown coat where Scott Mattaye had shot him through the chest. Scott remembered how a deer had fallen once that he had shot. He had shot wild fowl along the tidewater; he remembered how they fell, open-eyed, incurious, exactly as Mr. Still's eyes had opened, deep, incurious, staring into the light.

"Still!" said Scott, but he doubted if the man had ever heard him.

"Four aces," said Mr. Still. "The cards are falling my way, gentlemen....Sho, Henry, you'll not see me. I've sense enough for that....They're runnin'. There's no mistake. The whole thing's breakin'....Retreat? Why, it's a rout...and the cards are all my way....But I won't give you trouble, Henry. I know where I belong."

Then his head dropped sideways, and Scott had the intuition that the man was dead, as clear as knowledge, although it was the first time he had ever killed a man. Scott's head was swimming and his knees were weak. His left arm was bleeding at the shoulder. He tied it with his handkerchief, using his right hand and his teeth. Then he mounted and rode slowly toward the road. He had the colonel's message to deliver, but it no longer seemed important, now that he had killed.

"Sho, Henry," Mr. Still had said, "you'll not see me." And he was right. No one would see Mr. Still again.

The road was full of life. Teams of wounded were jolting toward the junction, and supply wagons were moving to the lines. Furtive, straggling men were plodding along the road, wandering like the lost soul of Mr. Still. All the demoralization of raw troops was there; he could imagine that the whole army was blundering and groping in the night, like a monster whose brains were very small.

It was hard to tell what had happened, once he reached Manassas, for the defense works were manned, and even at that late hour the town was in confusion. The main street was packed with wagons and stretchers, and with wounded propped against the picket fences waiting for the train. In contrast, headquarters was easy enough to find, because the confusion there seemed greater. A small frame house like all the others, it was like a beehive that night. Officers and messengers kept going in and out of the door like bees, and inside there was the same concentrated, humming sound.

"Wait a minute, sonny," a sentry said. "You can't go in there."

"Message," said Scott—"message for the general."

"Sonny," said the sentry, "what do you know of generals? This place is heavin' with generals. Why, the president himself's in yonder. You git used to generals here—and they don't know what they're doing any more'n you."

Then Scott heard a voice he knew: "Scott, what are you doing here this time of night?"

An officer was standing in the doorway. It was his brother-in-law, Hugh Fleece, on General Johnston's staff.

"Message for the general, sir," Scott said. "I had an accident on the road."

"You come inside," Hugh Fleece said. "I'll see someone in just a minute. You come inside and wait."

Plain people had lived in that house until a day or two before. The traces of their humdrum life were clashing with the staccato beat of mysterious forces. He was telling Hugh Fleece what had happened, in short, broken sentences, but even while he spoke his curiosity was strong. There was a small entry with narrow stairs and a dingy run of carpet; there was a chromo on the wall—Scott could remember it—of two dead partridges beside a dish of outrageous-looking fruit, but the space was full of tobacco smoke and voices, coming from rooms to the right and left. Though there had been no violence, some inviolate, quiet attribute of that house had been erased. All the level ties of humdrum life had been broken, and one could grasp the truth of war more clearly there than on a field where a thousand men had died.

Hugh Fleece himself was like that hall. The last time Scott Mattaye had seen him, Hugh Fleece had been in white linen and a broad straw hat. His face had been broad and good-humored, but now he was in a uniform from Lichtenstein's and his face was hard, confused and lined.

"Someone will want to question you," Hugh Fleece said. "This rout report is another of these rumors. Someone will want you. Lord knows who, with everything in such a devil of a mess and no one knowing what is what. Who sent this message—Stuart? Who the devil's Stuart? You'll have to wait. The generals are dining with the president, and no one even rightly knows who is the commanding general. It is all like that up here."

Voices, orderlies, officers shouldering in and out—the place was close and stuffy and as irrational as delirium.

"You're bleeding," said Hugh. "Your sleeve's all over blood."

The mention of his bleeding made Scott faint and dizzy.

"It's just a scratch," he said. "He only grazed me. I—I wish I hadn't killed that man. It—makes me feel right sick."

"You come upstairs," Hugh Fleece said. He was helping him up the stairs. "There's a bed up in our quarters. You lie down and wait. I'll have someone to see you, if anyone will listen....Were you in the fighting?...All right, Scott; I'll be back."

Scott should have known that Hugh Fleece would not come back. He should have known that no one would listen in the bedlam of that house.

Scott Mattaye was in a room beneath the eaves, where a lantern was burning very low. The place was strewn with overcoats and waterproof blankets, half covering a broken rocking-chair and a wide spool bed. There were religious mottoes on the wall, and he remembered one. "The Lord hears everything," it read.

Scott lay down upon the bed. He remembered that he almost fell, in a seizure of exhaustion. Then, when he closed his eyes to clear his thoughts, he saw the face of Mr. Still, just as he had seen it first—thoughtful, enigmatic and serene. It seemed to him sometimes that it was more than a memory—that the spirit of Mr. Still was standing there beside him, lips turned upward in that slow half smile.

He must have been asleep, because, when he opened his eyes, he was confused at first. There were voices, and it seemed to him that the room was full of people, but the voices were incredible. He could not believe he heard. The lantern was so low that the room was almost dark, but he could see that a door beside the bed had opened, letting in a clear, sharp light from an adjoining chamber. It was that adjoining room, not his, that was full of men and voices.

"Risk?" someone was saying, and whoever was speaking was angry. "Has it never come under your observation that war's made up of risk?"

"And don't forget, sir," someone answered, "that I'm the one who must consider it."

"And I tell you," the first voice said more loudly, "you're stopping upstairs here and talking, with the whole war in your hand. One mite of action tonight from a military man, and not a politician, and the South will win this war. You've whipped 'em, and has there been a bona fide effort to pursue? I ask you, has there?"

"General"—it was another voice—"I beg you won't forget you're addressing, among others, the president of the Confederate States of America."

There was a pause, and Scott Mattaye was sitting bolt upright, so startled that he could not move, for he knew what had happened. The adjoining room was full of generals, and the president was there, and Scott Mattaye was in that other room, listening like a spy.

He could feel the quietness of angry men, striving to keep cool. He could feel the presence of an imponderable question, hanging above them like a cloud.

"Thank you, sir," the first voice said. "I understand politics right well, and I'm right well aware whom I'm addressing, and the dangers I run for doing it; none of which impel me to take back a word."

"General," said someone.

"Sir," the first voice answered, "I'll say my say, and then I'll leave this room. I know you rank me, Joe, but just the same I repeat you held your hand short of victory. Will there be such a chance again, gentlemen? No, never! I've heard you talking—fool's talk. You think you've got the Yankee nation whipped and that Europe will intervene, because we've driven a passel of uniformed civilians across Bull Run. Gentlemen, don't you deceive yourselves! You don't know the Yankee nation if you think that—not you, Joe, or you, Beauregard, or you, Mr. President. Yonder northward is a power twice our strength, and they're no pack of cowards.

"You give that nation time, gentlemen, and we'll be crushed as sure as we're in this stuffy room. The sole hope for a weaker power is to wage offensive war. I heard General Jackson at the hospital. He said give him ten thousand men, and he'd be in Washington City, and, gentlemen, he's right. Take Washington, and Baltimore and Maryland will come over. Seize the coal fields and threaten Philadelphia. I repeat we've got 'em in our hands tonight if we dare to take risk. Do this, and we've smashed 'em, gentlemen.

"If supplies don't come up, live off the country. There's enough to feed us. If our army's disorganized, so's theirs. There's nothing to a defeated civilian army. Give Jackson those ten thousand. Give 'em to me tonight, and I'll have Washington for you, gentlemen. Follow up, and we've won this war. Wait here, and we whip ourselves. Thank you for listening, gentlemen. It's all I've got to say."

There was another pause, a slow, long silence. Scott could hear a chair creak; feet shuffled, someone struck a match; and then silence again.

"General," someone said, chillingly polite, "perhaps you have some information you have not divulged. This Northern disorganization you take as fact I do not believe exists. This enemy moved off quietly; his left was not engaged. How do you know he's whipped? We'd admire to hear you tell us, general."

"Intuition, gentlemen," the first voice answered—"a soldier's intuition, who's seen service and read military history; the intuition that makes an officer a leader. Jackson has that intuition. Gentlemen, green troops won't hold together when they're whipped. Longstreet had that intuition when he tried to give 'em canister this afternoon. Rely on intuition when information won't come in."

"Do you think, sir," someone said, "we'll risk our army and the war on the intuition of an ex-professor of the Institute?"

"Gentlemen," the first voice answered, "I'll wish you all good night, because I do not think you will. I've spoken out of duty what I believe the truth, but this I'll add: We'll live to see T.J. Jackson the greatest general of the South. I'll be going back to the lines. Good night, Mr. President. If plain talk has offended you, I'm sorry. Good night, gentlemen."

No one answered. Scott heard footsteps and the closing of a door, and the voice was gone—always a voice to him. It was gone into the limbo of memories, for he never heard that voice again, nor knew the owner of that voice. There was the same silence, heavy, dull. He could hear the rumble of wagons outside, teamsters calling and the crack of whips.

"If you want to have a good time," someone was singing outside—"a good time—"

It was the song that Stuart's cavalry sang, but the voice seemed very distant. A chair creaked again, and someone said:

"There goes another hot-head....What are we going to do?"

There was another pause; no answer.

"This is an unconfirmed report, gentlemen, that their retreat across Cub Run has degenerated into a panic, but we've only heard it from one source. Is Major Hill downstairs? Shall we call him up again?"

There was a hint of laughter, decorous and faint.

"Colonel," said someone, "will you fetch up Major Hill?"

There were footsteps again, and the closing of a door.

"If you want to have a good time." Scott could hear the voice outside singing the song again. Scott could feel himself being drawn nearer the door, for, in some strange way, the war had narrowed down to Scott Mattaye and the message in his hand.

"Here he is," said someone...."Major Hill, please repeat to us what you saw again."

"I said, sir," Scott could hear a voice stuttering with suppressed excitement, "the road was blocked with abandoned artillery and wagons. No one was there. I give you my word it's not a retreat but a rout, sir. There's no resistance. There's—"

"Thank you," someone interrupted; "that will do." And there was another silence.

"May I ask who is that officer?"

"He's on my staff, Mr. President," came the answer. "One of the Hills, sir—old army. Come to think of it, he goes by the name of Crazy Hill."

The tenseness seemed to relax again into a faint hint of mirth. "Crazy Hill—why do they call him that?"

"A nickname from the academy, Mr. President, gained from his manner, but there has been no reflection on his conduct or intelligence."

"And all we have to rely on tonight is the report of Crazy Hill?"

It seemed to Scott that his blood was congealed, but he knew he could not wait. He pulled on the half-opened door, and next he was standing in a small room lighted by a lamp placed on the center of a deal table. Maps were on the table—heaps of maps and papers. There were perhaps eight men seated around this table, tired, stained officers with heavy beards and mustaches, but Scott Mattaye could never recollect the number or get their faces straight. They were all in the uniforms of generals or staff officers except one, who wore a black frock coat, setting off a slender, well-proportioned figure. His face was clean-shaven and handsome, a proud, self-conscious face. The nose was very straight; the lips were thin. Scott had seen him in the distance once, and Scott knew who he was—Jefferson Davis, president of the Confederate States of America.

"Beg pardon, sir," Scott said, and he began to stutter exactly like Crazy Hill. "I have a message for the general. I was waiting, but I thought he ought to see it, sir."

"Colonel"—a general officer, a short, peppery-looking man, half rose from his chair—"what's all this? Who let this fool in here?"

Scott flushed. He was still young enough in those days not to be awed by rank.

"I was told to wait here," he said, "in the room yonder, until someone could see me about a message I was to deliver to the general, and I've waited a right long time. I'm from Colonel Stuart, sir, with a message for General Johnston. A man from Centerville came to our picket, sir, with news the Yankees are running. There's not a fighting force between here and Washington, he said. And when I heard the gentlemen speaking—I'm not a fool, general, if you please."

Everyone was staring at him. He saw the general's face grow red.

"Damnation," said the general. "Have you been listening at the door? What idiot let you up here, and what's your name?"

Scott Mattaye stood up straighter, and the implication in the general's tone made him speak out plainly:

"I'm Mattaye, sir—Scott Mattaye from Deer Bottom. I was put in that next room and told to wait. It wasn't my fault the door came open, sir. If I've heard anything I should not have heard, I shall be pleased to go outside and shoot myself, sir. It's all that I can do."

He thought they were impressed by what he said, for their expressions had subtly changed.

"The Mattayes?" The president was speaking. "Of course. I know the family. He sounds like a Mattaye."

The general leaned back in his chair. "He sounds as sensible as half the nation," he said. "Wouldn't you be better pleased to keep your mouth shut, or would you rather shoot yourself?"

Then everyone was laughing, as though something in the room had snapped, bursting into strands of mirth.

Scott Mattaye had never been ashamed as he was then, for he had spoken as a gentleman, according to his best tradition. Another general officer had risen from the table— also small, with delicately formed hands—and he walked toward Scott Mattaye with quick, neat steps.

"Excuse!" he said in a slightly foreign accent. "There is General Johnston. Give him your message, please."

They had spread the message on the table, and next they were reading it over one another's shoulders.

"He's right," someone said. "They're running like a pack of hounds. Why didn't we get this before? Who kept this man waiting?"

No one answered, and even Scott Mattaye could see that the confusion of the army was in that room, with no one who could call for order.

"'Man forwarded for questioning,'" said someone, reading from the message. "Well, where is he, trooper?"

They would have been pleased to see him dead if he could have brought in Mr. Still alive.

"Man, where's your prisoner? Did you leave him with the guard?"

"He's dead," said Scott Mattaye. "I killed him."

"Killed him!" someone shouted. "Do you know what you've done? You've killed the only man who's seen the Yankees running!"

Then it seemed to Scott Mattaye that Mr. Still was there. He could have sworn that the shade of Mr. Still was standing just beside him.

"I reckon I couldn't help it," said Scott Mattaye. "It was him or me. He had a pistol on me. He tried to get away."

"Nonsense," said someone. "He had valuable information. Why should he try to get away?"

"He was wanted south, sir," Scott answered. "He was afraid that someone here would know him and I reckon he was proud. He was a gambling man."

Then, across the table, Scott saw the face of a staff colonel. He had not noticed the officer before, but now that Scott saw him, he stood out beyond all the other figures in that room. It seemed to Scott that he was looking straight into the eyes of Mr. Still, though Mr. Still was dead.

"A gambler, you said?" The officer was speaking. His eyes were deep and dark like Mr. Still's. Scott never knew his name. "Did this man say who he was?"

"He gave the name of Still, sir," Scott answered—"Jack Still."

A pale light flickered across the colonel's face, but his expression did not change.

"I see he touched you in the arm. A dark, thin man?"

"Yes, sir," said Scott, and their eyes met for an instant, and Scott could read the other's eyes as clearly as a printed page.

"Don't tell," the eyes were saying—"don't tell any more."

"Gentlemen"—the officer cleared his throat—"I knew this man. He was dangerous, and of course the trooper only did what's right. But I'll say this: I knew Jack Still. If he said the Yankees were running, you can believe that message every word, because I knew Jack Still."

"Colonel," someone asked, "he knew you were back here?"

The colonel's voice was smooth as velvet, and slow and peaceful like that other voice.

"Yes, sir," he answered, "I reckon that he knew."

Then the president was speaking, and Scott Mattaye was never sure, but sometimes he thought that the president's voice was changed:

"Gentlemen, we can't talk here all night. If the trooper will go into the next room and close the door, I should like to see him later."

Then Scott was standing in lantern light, where the closed door shut off the distinctness of the voices, which were sometimes faint and sometimes loud.

"Don't tell," the officer's eyes were saying—"don't tell any more."

His thoughts were all confusion, like the battle and the army and the sounds beyond the door. He had only heard half secrets, but the talk of armies moving was nothing to the expression on that one man's face.

"I see he touched you in the arm," the officer had said. "A dark, thin man?"

"Yes, sir." And Scott had nearly added: "About your height and build."

He had not realized what had made him stop, but he knew, now that he was alone. He had stopped from instinctive delicacy, because that colonel of the staff resembled Mr. Still. Their height and build, their eyes and voices were alike. He had not spoken of such a matter, and he would not, because no gentleman would speak.

It must have been half an hour later when he heard a tapping on the door.

"Trooper"—he knew the voice—"you may come in now."

When Scott came in, the president was standing in the room alone. The chairs were pushed back from the table, empty, but the maps and papers were still there.

"Sir?" said Scott Mattaye, but Mr. Davis was not looking at him. "Did you call me, sir?"

The president was holding a paper in his hand, and he did not appear to have heard Scott speak, for he seemed removed from everything except from his own mind. Before he answered he tore the paper once across the center, gathered the pieces and tore them once again. Then he looked at Scott Mattaye and smiled. He had a winning, pleasant smile.

"Do you know what I've torn up?" he asked, just as though he and Scott were friends.

"No, sir," Scott answered.

The president looked at him for a moment. He had level eyes; his forehead was wide and fine.

"But you can guess?" he said.

He could guess, although he did not answer, and the president seemed pleased.

"Very well, if you can guess, I'll tell you. I've torn up the orders for immediate pursuit. Some day you can tell your children that you very nearly made the army move tonight—very nearly, with the information of a gambler, backed by a man named Crazy Hill. You'll never know all the circumstances. I may be wrong, but I'm not a gambling man."

Scott Mattaye did not answer. That burst of frankness could surprise him still, for he could never explain it, except that the man was obliged to speak to someone through some reflex of emotion. He came to know that there were times when anyone must speak.

"No," said the president again, "I'm not a gambling man, Mattaye."

"Yes, sir," answered Scott, and he knew that the president was not a gambling man.

"That man—your prisoner—did he resemble anyone in this room?"

"No, sir," answered Scott; "not that I remember."

"The officer who spoke to you"—the president clasped his hands behind his back—"was moved; he was under an emotion. Was there no resemblance?"

"No, sir," answered Scott; "none that I remember."

The president had seen exactly what he had seen, and the knowledge passed wordlessly between them.

"Mattaye, I like a man who can't remember. You understand? I know you understand. There are circumstances one must not remember after they have happened. Shall we call this one? I like a man who can forget, and I should be very pleased to have you in my family."

"Your family, sir?" said Scott, and the president smiled again.

"Not as a private, Mattaye, but as an officer who can see. There were men here tonight who did not like me, and you could see. I shall be plainer later, but I repeat I've watched you, and I have the intuition that you will be very useful. I should be glad to have you in my family as an aide."

"But why, sir?" Scott asked him. "Why do you want me?"

The president stepped closer to him and lowered his voice:

"Because your prisoner was a brother of an officer in this room. You knew, and you saved the pain of making it obvious, because you are a gentleman."

The president was waiting. Scott looked down at his uniform, bleached by the sun already, and misshapen by the weather. The president was waiting and the room was hot and still. He could hear the wagons outside. "If you want to have a good time—a good time—" The echo of the song he had heard was moving through his mind. The cavalry— there were no subtleties or secrets in the cavalry. Out on the edge of the army, Jeb Stuart could say what he felt and thought, without caution, without fear. There were no rooms or voices on outpost with the cavalry. He looked at the president again, in his black frock coat—neat, precise and poised. "If you want to have a good time—" The president was waiting.

"Is that an order, sir?" asked Scott Mattaye.

"No." The other seemed surprised. "An invitation, not an order."

"Then, sir," said Scott, "if it's no order, I'd prefer—I'm much honored, sir, but I'd rather be out with the cavalry."

There was no resentment in the cavalry, or spite, such as Scott saw for an instant before that slim man turned away. He had held the war in his hand, and had dropped it, and Scott knew why—because he was not great enough to hold a war.

"Very well," he replied. "I see I was mistaken. Go back with the cavalry."

A Debt of Honor

F. SCOTT FITZGERALD

"Prayle!"

"Here."

"Martin!"

"Absent."

"Sanderson!"

"Here."

"Carlton, for sentry duty!"

"Sick."

"Any volunteers to take his place?"

"Me, me," said Jack Sanderson, eagerly.

"All right," said the captain and went on with the roll.

It was a very cold night. Jack never quite knew how it came about. He had been wounded in the hand the day before and his gray jacket was stained a bright red where he had been hit by a stray ball. And "number six" was such a long post. From way up by the general's tent to way down by the lake. He could feel a faintness stealing over him. He was very tired and it was getting very dark—very dark.

They found him there, sound asleep, in the morning worn out by the fatigue of the march and the fight which had followed it. There was nothing the matter with him save the wounds, which were slight, and military rules were very strict. To the last day of his life Jack always remembered the sorrow in his captain's voice as he read aloud the dismal order.

Camp Bowling Green, C.S.A. Jan. 15, 1863, U.S.

For falling asleep while in a position of trust at a sentry post, private John Sanderson is hereby condemned to be shot at sunrise on Jan. 16, 1863.
> *By order of*
> *Robert E. Lee,*
> *Lieutenant General Commanding*

Jack never forgot the dismal night and the march which followed it. They tied a handkerchief over his head and led him a little apart to a wall which bounded one side of the camp. Never had life seemed so sweet.

General Lee in his tent thought long and seriously upon the matter.

"He is so awfully young and of good family too; but camp discipline must be enforced. Still it was not much of an offense for such a punishment. The lad was over tired and wounded. By George, he shall go free if I risk my reputation. Sergeant, order private John Sanderson to be brought before me."

"Very well, sir," and saluting, the orderly left the tent.

Jack was brought in, supported by two soldiers, for a reaction had set in after his narrow escape from death.

"Sir," said General Lee sternly, "on account of your extreme youth you will get off with a reprimand but see that it never happens again, for, if it should, I shall not be so lenient."

"General," answered Jack drawing himself up to his full height, "the Confederate States of America shall never have cause to regret that I was not shot;" and Jack was led away, still trembling, but happy in the knowledge of a new found life.

Six weeks after with Lee's army near Chancellorsville. The success of Fredericksburg had made possible this advance of the Confederate arms. The firing had just commenced when a courier rode up to General Jackson.

"Colonel Barrows says, sir, that the enemy have possession of a small frame house on the outskirts of the woods and it overlooks our earthworks. Has he your permission to take it by assault?"

"My compliments to Colonel Barrows and say that I cannot spare more than twenty men but that he is welcome to charge with that number," answered the General.

"Yes, sir," and the orderly, setting spurs to his horse, rode away.

Five minutes later a column of men from the 3rd Virginia burst out from the woods and ran toward the house. A galling fire broke out from the Federal lines and many a brave man fell, among whom was their leader, a young lieutenant. Jack Sanderson sprang to the front and waving his gun encouraged the men onward. Half way between the Confederate lines and the house was a small mound, and behind this the men threw themselves to get a minute's respite.

A minute later a figure sprang up and ran toward the house, and before the Union troops saw him he was half way across the bullet swept clearing. Then the federal fire was directed at him. He staggered for a moment and placed his hand to his forehead. On he ran and reaching the house he quickly opened the door and went inside. A minute later a pillar of flame shot out of the windows of the house and almost immediately afterwards the Federal occupants were in full flight. A long cheer rolled along the Confederate lines and then the word was given to charge and they charged sweeping all before them. That night the searchers wended their way to the half burned house. There on the floor, beside the mattress he had set on fire, lay the body of him who had once been John Sanderson, private, third Virginia. He had paid his debt.

O Captain! My Captain!

H. Bedford–Jones

Jeff Mindlery sat patching the sole of a brogan with a strip of cowhide. He was a stalwart, serious young fellow, shaggily towheaded, in flop-brimmed slouch hat and ragged Confederate gray. The downy chin-stubble of his lean face wagged, as he champed on his comforter of Virginia twist, and listened to the talk around him, while cobbling earnestly.

The rains, marking the first week in April, were past. It was close to noon of the first day of May; a downright pleasant day, warmish with Virginia's springtime sun. Here the great camp of the Army of Northern Virginia lay fronting the west and the Wilderness.

Smoke from thousands of mess fires hazed the air over the heights of Fredericksburg beside the Rappahannock, drifting across town and valley, hanging above the western slopes and lowlands. The air was hazy in all directions, for a long distance. Cannon and musketry lent their fumes to the haze, but the rattle of skirmish fire had died out.

A scowl touched Mindlery's face as a voice near by bawled out a verse of what was, to the young South Carolinian, a ribald song:

> He's riding past, the old slouch hat
> Cocked o'er his eye askew,
> The shrewd, dry smile, the speech so pat,
> So calm, so blunt, so true!

> Each Yankee leader he can tell;
> Says he: "That's Banks! He's fond of shell.
> Lord save his soul! We'll give him—" Well,
>   That's Stonewall Jackson's way.

Mindlery disapproved such words; he took his commander seriously.

Glancing about as he cobbled, the regimental flag caught his eye, and pride rose in him. It was laid from one stack of muskets to another; along the droop of its folds showed a hint of South Carolina's palmetto; a once handsome flag, embroidered by home hands, but now frayed and stained and shot-rent.

"Twenty mile by moonshine in eight hour, up hill an' down through the brush," said one of the lounging men beside Mindlery. "And hyar we be. Old Jack's foot cavalry."

Another grunted. "Huh? Last fall, when we took Harper's Ferry, it was eighty mile in three days; and fifteen mile in four hours to Antietam. He is shorely powerful hard on shoe leather."

"But he's powerful tough in a fight." Jeff Mindlery turned to Tom Sewall, and held up the worn brogan. "Well, she's patched, best I can. Where do we go next, Tom?"

"Whar do we go next?" Lying on his side, Sewall eased his long flank, took the pipe from his russet beard, and spat. "We go whar Stonewall Jackson starts us goin'; jest set out, and right soon we jump the Yanks and lick 'em. That's the Bible of it."

Mindlery gave a sober nod. "He shorely is a power in religion, too. He reckons he's a soldier of the Lord, app'inted by Gawd Almighty to free the South for her rights."

"Did you fellers ever see him," spoke up Sewall, "standin' with one arm raised straight up, signalin' to the Almighty? 'Here I be, Lord, Stonewall Jackson, of Stonewall's corps, with the Bible and the sword of Gideon, ready to smite!' That's him."

"Yeah," said another. "I hear tell one arm is heavier than the other, so he lifts it to let the blood flow down out of it and ekilize it. Shorely is heavy enough when it falls on the Yanks! But he don't tolerate any heavy feet."

Here there rose a laugh, though Jeff did not join in it. He was frowning reflectively. Sewall, who was something of an oracle, spat again and delivered his opinion.

"Right now Old Jack is out to the front with them other scouting divisions of ours; but you can bet the rest of us warn't fetched here in a hurry to set and cool our heels. When he comes in, he'll tell General Lee what he reckons is to be done. Then we'll have a leetle session of prayer; then we'll go along with him and do it."

"That's right," said someone else. "What about the last couple o' days' fighting, Tom?"

"Oh, that's clear," Sewall rejoined. "The Yanks threwed some troops acrost the river down below, to draw attention; their main body crossed up above. Now they're hived at Chancellorsville, holding the roads and most of the fords. General Lee got a mite fooled there. Now the Yanks allow they got us between the river and the Wilderness, and can cut us off from Richmond."

"Who's the gin'ral over yonder?" somebody inquired.

"Joe Hooker himself," Sewall replied. "Well, we got Lee, and Jeb Stuart's horse cavalry, and Old Jack's foot cavalry; and I reckon Old Jack can persuade Gawd Almighty to lay off helping Joe Hooker a spell—"

"You hadn't ought to joke about that, Tom," Jeff Mindlery put in very gravely. "It don't sound right, to make a joke about Old Jack. I love that man, like I'd love a woman; and I got a woman waiting back home whom I love mighty well. I'm aiming to name my next young 'un Jackson Stonewall."

Tom Sewall spat again. "That proclamation by Abe Lincoln to free and arm the blacks is like to end the war and send you home suddener than you'd think, Jeff. A heap of men on the other side are fightin' to keep the South in the Union; but they won't fight to rob us of our rightful property. Wait and see. What you scowling about, anyhow?"

"Thinking," said Mindlery. "I got a brother, Dick, who moved up into Pennsylvany a long while back. He's fighting on the other side. I hear this Yank Army of the Potomac has got Pennsylvany troops. How do I know but what a bullet I shoot will kill Dick?"

"That's a bad thing to worry about," said Sewall sympathetically, "but I guess a sight of us worry about it. Lots of us got kin on t'other side. Any bullet is liable to kill some man the shooter sets store by."

"This war looks to me," said Mindlery, "like murder to orders."

"Well, aint we fighting for our rights, Jeff?"

"I reckon. But I was raised religious, not to shed the blood of any human," said Jeff Mindlery with earnest pondering. "When South Carolina went out, I held off; I got a wife and three young 'uns to look after. Then the conscription started in to comb the country. Anyone who offered himself without bein' drawn could elect where he'd like to serve. I come to j'in Jackson, the Blue-light general, 'cause my folks are all Blue-light Presbyterians.

"He wouldn't pray so strong," he went on, "if he wasn't in the right. When I see Old Jack squinting from under his hat, or signalin' the Almighty with his arm held up, I feel like I'm fighting so's not to disapp'int Stonewall Jackson. Far as I'm concerned, danged if he aint the hull Confederate States of America!"

> *Silence! Ground arms! Kneel all—caps off,*
> *Old Blue-light's going to pray.*
> *Strangle the fool who dares to scoff.*
> *"Attention!" hear him say,*
> *Appealing from his native sod*
> *In forma pauperis to God:*
> *"Lay bare Thine arm, stretch forth Thy rod!*
> *"Amen!" That's Stonewall's way.*

The afternoon dragged on and passed; the last skirmish, out in the woods to the front, was ended. The sunset air quieted; and undisturbed, Jeff Mindlery concluded the letter he was writing home. He read over the scrawl, his blue eyes puckered and his lips moving:

> *Camp near Fredericksburg, Va.*
> *May 1, 1863.*

> *Dearest Lizzie:*
>   *We are still here where we been all winter, but this morning early Old Jack marched us upriver a piece of twenty mile and set us out in front of General Lee's part of the army, in the woods over against the Wilderness. The Yanks of their general, Joe Hooker, took a notion to come across to our side by fords, and I hear tell they are holed in a place called Chancellorsville. I reckon they*

*fooled General Lee by doing some shooting downriver
while the main parcel crossed upriver. Some of our boys
had a smart scrimmage this afternoon on the turnpike
road to Chancellorsville with Yanks who were coming
clean out, and made them change their minds. We got
around 70,000 men and they got near 120,000, but we
got God and Old Jack, so don't you worry. I am all right
except for shoes and a vast hankering to see you and the
young ones. Us foot cavalry are liable to go somewhere
mighty sudden and smoke those Yanks out of their cover.
God bless and keep you all till—*

His reading disturbed, he glanced aside as Tom Sewall
plumped himself down.

"Where you been, Tom? Got any news?"

"Some of us been visiting that Virginny regiment next
to us. Thar's a meeting at headquarters, with Old Jack and
General Lee settin' on cracker boxes, argyfying."

Mindlery nodded. "That means we get called to prayer,
then get quickstep orders and be off to find the Yanks."

"I reckon so. A Virginny man was acting messenger at
headquarters. He heard Old Jack say: 'I'll make the try with
my whole corps present.' That means nigh a third of the
army, and I reckon us foot cavalry will do a march around
to catch 'em unsuspected; that's Stonewall's way."

"Well," said Mindlery, "I'll sign this letter home, and
then hold it for a postscript. Nope; might's well add it right
now: *'God and Old Jack and us have licked 'em again.'* I'll get
it off later."

He finished his scribble, and pocketed it. The twilight
waned; the lines of gray and butternut got their supper. Then
came sudden orders in the dusk. *"Attention!"*

The ranks formed without arms. The chaplains were out;
a group of horsemen rode along the center, the leader sitting
loosely in the saddle. Despite West Point training, he rode
with the heavy seat of a Virginia farmer.

A well-knit, muscular man in jackboots, gray frock coat
with the collar insignia of a lieutenant general, and broad
slouch hat, this. A man of dark full beard slightly grizzled,
long head and commanding straight nose, and deeply glowing gray eyes—a countenance rugged, grave, somewhat
austere. When he removed his hat, his forehead showed
high and majestic. He was, to all these men, a certain sign

of battle. Jeff Mindlery shifted feet and wet his lips, as the lifted arm silenced the cheers. Jackson's voice came rolling:

"Before we march to rout the enemy again by the help of the Lord of Hosts, let us bare our heads and give thanks for the power to smite. I want you all to join with me in humble prayer to the Almighty."

Drooping his beard on his chest, the General closed his eyes and prayed in a sonorous voice; his staff and the foot officers and ranks awaited the "Amen," and swelled it in a responsive murmur. Jackson, as though in firm assurance that the enemy were to be smitten hip and thigh, raised his head, straightened in the saddle, restored his hat, and flashed his eye along the line. Eager voices broke out.

"Where you fixing to take us, General?"

"Into the Wilderness a piece, boys. But I'll bring you out, so trust in God and obey orders."

"Three cheers for Old Jack!"

His arm lifted. "Do your yelling when you charge the enemy."

"You do the praying, and we'll do the fighting!" blurted out Tom Sewall; amid a burst of laughter, the General rode on to other divisions.

Ranks were dismissed; the orders were to rest, but be ready to move. Pioneers vanished into the woods that hedged the western road to Chancellorsville. Mindlery listened for the whanging sounds of the axes, punctuating the night air, while fragments of gossip floated from the men around him.

"Them axes are clearin' the way to somewheres for us!"

"Old Jack cl'ared the way when he prayed like a Blue-light elder at a revival meeting! He knows what he aims to do, and done told Gawd about it."

"Aint told the Yanks, though," said Tom Sewall dryly. "Only him and Gawd and General Lee know what's up. Us and the Yanks will find out. Eh, Jeff?"

Mindlery blinked solemnly. "Yes, I reckon, Tom. I declare again, I shorely do love that man! When he orders me to shoot at other men, he's likely in the right about it."

This idea relieved his worry. After all, he was a simple young fellow, and visioned things around him with simple candor.

The moon rose. It looked down upon valleyed Fredericksburg, on the Rappahannock wending southeastward, and the Army of Northern Virginia, foot, horse, and artillery, the earthworks and log breastworks, the stacked arms, the picketed mounts, the batteries watchful of the river, the hostile west and the vague Wilderness.

It looked down on the Turnpike and the branching Plank Road to Chancellorsville, the old Chancellor house, the Army of the Potomac, foot, horse and artillery, the stacked arms, the parked mounts, the batteries whose wings extended to the rear in a curve on either flank.

Jeff Mindlery roused to reveille at daylight; he roused to roll-call, coffee and cornbread. "Fall in!...Count off!... Column of fours—march!"

> *He's in the saddle now. Fall in!*
> *Steady, the whole brigade!*
> *Hill's at the ford, cut off; we'll win*
> *Him clear, by ball and blade!*
> *What matter if our shoes are worn?*
> *What matter bloody feet and torn?*
> *Quickstep! We'll join him ere the morn—*
> *That's Stonewall Jackson's way!*

The column took to the Turnpike, struck to the left for the Plank Road branch, and quit that for the woods. At midday twenty thousand men in a long column were winding through the overgrown tobacco fields, the hazel and sassafras, the oaks and pines, of the Wilderness. They halted to close up, while the Pioneers cleared the road anew. They trudged again, into ravines and out. Mindlery and his friend sweated along together.

"We're heading cl'ar around the Yanks," panted Tom Sewall. "That's Old Jack's way: start in at one spot and come out at another!"

Mindlery frowned uneasily. "What I'd like to know, are any Pennsylvany troops where we come out."

"A Yank's a Yank, don't matter where from."

"A man don't like to be shooting maybe his own brother."

"This is war, Jeff. When you let go, you can't tell who you're going to hit."

"I can, most always," said Mindlery.

Gunfire sounded on the right and to the rear. Jeb Stuart's horse was riding the flank; the wagon train was behind; the main column never faced about. Yanks had sallied into the brush, but they were too late to head off the march. By the distant rumbling, Lee's artillery seemed to be drawing attention to itself by way of diversion.

Deer, foxes, partridges and rabbits bolted from their coverts, to be speeded by genial view-halloo's. Jeff Mindlery's feet were hot; his tongue was dry. The distant firing was now smothered by the woods and thickets, as the sun slanted in from the west.

The column picked up the Turnpike and headed on through the Wilderness; with a right half wheel it was turning back, as if for Fredericksburg again—but now the Yanks and Chancellorsville lay in between. Jeff Mindlery turned to his companion.

"Who's the Yank general we'll lick first?"

"Howard, I reckon," Sewall replied. "The one who lost an arm at Fair Oaks, a year ago—and serve him right for fighting on the wrong side! This time, he'll lose his shirt."

"I'd hate to be the man who lost him his arm," said Mindlery soberly. "I don't see much glory in mangling folks, but I reckon Old Jack knows best."

Silence! No talking. Shuffle, shuffle, down the road to Chancellorsville. Stonewall Jackson was marching in, and nobody there knew it. Fifteen miles roundabout through the brush; twenty thousand men afoot with no turning back; seventy thousand Yanks ahead.

Now the low sun shone hotly on the back of Mindlery's neck. From the advance came Stonewall himself at a trot, riding down the column with arm and hand uplifted and a high look on his face as though listening to the Lord. No cheers, no cheers! He was inspecting his boys.

Halt! Orders crackled; the divisions were reformed in three lines, crossing the Turnpike and filing out into the woods and brush on either flank. The rumor spread that the picnic was only a mile or so ahead. An aide from the colonel was talking with Captain Harley, who turned and came searching along the line of men.

"The General wants a little scouting done. Sewall, you take Mindlery and scout on ahead till you can see what the Yanks are doing. Mind they don't sight you. Watch out for pickets. Get back quickly and report to the General."

"Old Jack can depend on South Car'lina," responded Sewall jauntily.

Mindlery stepped out with him. With muskets carried at will, they headed through the woods skirting the road. The sun cast long shadows; the quiet of eventide was due, but the trees were uneasy. Figures of wild things flitted and scurried.

"Them danged deer make more noise than we do," grumbled Mindlery. "No pickets out, anyhow."

Presently came the tang of woodsmoke and the hum of voices. Sewall hesitated, and plucked at his russet mop. "That thar knoll," he muttered. "You shin up a tree." They dodged forward like hunters to the little rise, and Mindlery climbed a handy tree.

Across a clearing were log and brush breastworks; beyond these, a host of bluecoats. Here were fires, stacked arms, knots of soldiers—the Yanks were getting supper. The nearest of them were within easy range. A group was singing:

Old Joe Hooker come out of the Wilderness,
Out of the Wilderness, out of the—

The level rays of light made every detail clear. Jeff Mindlery stared, started, caught his breath. Then, swallowing hard, he carefully descended and turned upon the back trail. The blue host had not seen them and would not hear them now. Mindlery heard his own voice bursting with uneven, quivering accents of emotion.

"My Gawd, Tom! I dassn't fire into them Yanks! I seen him plain—my brother Dick!"

"Sho', Jeff!" Sewall shook his head. "You don't mean it! Certain it was him?"

"No mistake. I told you Dick was with the Pennsylvany troops."

"Well, aint your fault," said Sewall. "Take Old Jack, now. He was raised in western Virginny, that's mostly gone Union, and married a Northern lady to boot. They say it come right hard to choose sides."

"I won't fire into them Yanks, I tell you!" Mindlery gulped.

"Shucks, Jeff, you don't stand no big chance of killing your brother! Wouldn't know it if you did. You aint fighting him, anyhow. Like as not we'll capture him along with the rest, and he'll be safe till the war's over."

"Well, I won't fire," Mindlery said stubbornly. "I'll charge with the bayonet, but I won't shoot! I'll see what I'm doing. I won't take chances of killing blind."

"Oh, dang you and your brother!" Sewall said irritably. "Come on! Shake a leg!"

The General heard the report, nodded gravely, and stroked his beard. The colors were draped at one side—not the Stars and Bars of the Confederacy, which had more than once been confused with the Stars and Stripes in the field, but the purely unofficial flag with the thirteen stars on a blue St. Andrew's cross on a red ground. The Battle Flag, it was called. There was something brave and splendid and reckless about it; the whole army had taken to it with a savage pride.

The General nodded again, as with certainty. His two tired eyes cleft by the straight nose seemed to vision things afar and bring them near. A flash lit them and died again. Stonewall,—Old Jack,—who looked first to the Lord and General Lee, then looked up the Yanks, saw clear triumph within his grasp, and once more nodded as though pleased. With a quick twist of his bearded lips he smiled and spoke.

"Very well. Howard and his Eleventh Corps are delivered to us. In twenty-four hours General Hooker will come out of the Wilderness indeed—at the bidding of General Lee. I suppose you boys are all hungry? Well, you know where to get a warm supper."

Forward, march! Guide center! No noise!

The advance division moved down the Turnpike and through the woods, at easy shuffling stride, slouch hats pulled down, muskets at the ready, eyes glittering ahead.

"What a sight of game! Look at it!" muttered Mindlery. Low comment ran along the breasting line. Fur and feather darted here and there amid the sunset shadows; deer went bounding, trapped by the extended flanks closing in on a two-mile front.

"We furnish the meat and the Yanks will do the cooking," breathed someone. Luther Jones, it was, a Charleston man. But Jeff Mindlery, breath short and pulses beating, heard his own voice make low comment:

"They won't have time to cook this meat. We're most there."

Shuffle, shuffle—mind how you set your feet! Some of those Yanks may have ears. Again came the tang of wood-fires, the hum of voices. Mindlery glimpsed the clearing. He saw deer go bounding, leaping the breastworks and bolting on for the farther brush, while blue figures turned and stared. Then the signal bugle blared.

"That's it!" Tom Sewall burst out.

The line of men flowed forward. The fringe of muskets leaped and belched in a roar. The men in gray plunged into the smoke, a shrilly vibrant yell pealing up. Far to right and left the files burst from the trees, legs and lungs working, muskets spouting again.

Over the ramparts now, over and into the camp! The Yanks here were running and shouting. They tried to form up, sprang for the stacked arms. Mindlery saw the whitened and bearded faces, the moiling figures, the gesturing officers with swords drawn; then he saw the rout, blue figures swept on before the smoke and bayonets and the storm of men. Figures staggering, falling, scampering, shouldering into forming ranks behind and scattering them wildly.

All was confusion, to Jeff. There went Old Jack at the gallop, leaning forward, his hat-brim glaring. The lulls shuddered with the vibrant mutter of distant guns, Lee's guns, pounding at the enemy's far left while Old Jack crowded back the right, here. Jeff Mindlery's musket was cold in his hands. No sign of his brother Dick.

The Yanks made a stand with infantry and artillery; but the second gray line came in with a wild yell, and the stand broke.

The sun was gone now; the smoke thinned; exultant voices brayed all around Mindlery. Masses of Yanks and wagons in full flight, they said. The right wing of Hooker's army pushed in on the center. Old Jack had advanced beyond the camp; tomorrow Hooker would be pinched to a finish between Old Jack and Lee. Chancellorsville was only a mile and a half distant, by road. So ran the eager tongues.

The recall sounded, and the skirmishers drifted back.

The sun's bright lances rout the mists
Of mourning—and by George!
Here's Longstreet struggling in the lists,
Hemmed in an ugly gorge
By Pope's brigade, whipped once before!
"Bay'nets and grape!" hear Stonewall roar.
"Charge, Stuart! Pay off Ashby's score
In Stonewall Jackson's way!"

The panting men gathered; the lines had to be reformed for the night. The Yanks were licked, but might not stay licked.

The woods, where South Carolina lay in position with pickets out, were seeping with acrid powder-fumes. To the north was the Turnpike, to the south the abandoned old Plank Road. The moonlit rifts in the thickets were misty. Gunfire boomed sullenly in the east, where Lee kept at work, and occasionally burst more closely, as Union artillery hammered the woods to cover the retreat.

Jeff Mindlery, posted in an advanced picket with Sewall, Luther Jones and others, was hungry.

"I'd like a chance at some o' that Yank grub," he said wistfully.

"Sore feet and empty bellies and the Yanks on the run—that's Old Jack's way," said Jones, with a harsh laugh. All of them felt exultant, drunk with fight and triumph.

"I'm glad I put that postscript on my letter, anyhow," Mindlery declared. "Listen! Aint it terrible, back there?"

They all paused, catching the cries and groans of the wounded. Jeff grunted under his breath.

"Aint on my hands. If I knew my brother wasn't hurt," went on Mindlery, "I'd rest tol'able easy. I didn't let go once."

"I dunno what I did, myself," Sewall said. "I just whanged away and yelled. Them Yanks never did me any harm, personal. War's a killing business, any way you look at it. Old Jack knows that. He don't ask the Lord to spare. He asks to get there first and hit hardest."

"I reckon the Yanks think they're fighting for the right too," Mindlery said moodily. "Well, I'm satisfied with Stonewall Jackson. If he says it's right, so it is."

Luther Jones stirred uneasily. "Aint this a grand night for a coon hunt? Wisht I was home with the dawgs, treeing a coon."

"The trees around hyar are right low-branching," Sewall declared. "You could climb up and shake out a coon in no time. Where I come from, it's taller. Sometimes we have to shoot the varmint out, given light enough to draw a bead on him."

Jones bit off a chew. "That's uncertain with a torch to shine him with. This hazy kind o' moon, full o' shadders, is uncertain too. It's amazing how a feller can miss when he pulls off, even if he draws a bead."

"Shucks! I don't miss, and I don't draw any bead," said Jeff Mindlery, who was proud of his shooting. "When it comes to night shooting, I let go by feel. If somebody shines the varmint's eyes, or I can get a glimpse of him, I calculate to fetch him first shot, bead or no bead. I point like I'd point a finger."

The moon rose higher. The smoky mist settled into the hollows. The openings among the trees cleared to short vistas cut by black shadow. The air was still, lifeless. Firing died out entirely; the appeals from the wounded lapsed, as search parties got to work. The picket guard rested, smoked, muttered.

"Them Yanks are up to something," said Sewall confidently. "They got plenty men and don't have to take this licking. But Old Jack knows. If the Yanks come cooning, he'll be all ready for 'em."

"We only used part o' the corps," said someone. "That third line didn't come up."

"That's what we're waiting for," Sewall rejoined. "Old Jack is done praying, this spell. He'll push on to hold that ford acrost the Rappahannock in the Yanks' rear; then they'll be pinched right."

"Where's their cavalry?" Mindlery demanded. "I hear they got a host o' cavalry, but all we've seen were infantry."

Luther Jones spat. "They can't whip this corps with cavalry in the woods, but they may fetch some up to reconnoiter. If they do, there'll be empty saddles. You heard the orders—fire if we see any."

Sewall nudged Jeff Mindlery. "I reckon you'll fire into Yank cavalry, huh? You wouldn't hold back on that."

"Oh, sure. You all know I don't aim to hold back," said Mindlery. "If I'm minded to shoot for Old Jack, I'll shoot; he's pious, and he'd tell me right. I dunno but what I'd shoot at my brother if he says it's right. Still, I don't want to go home feeling that maybe I've killed Dick unbeknown. When I'm suspicious that he's in front of me, I can't take the chance. It's different, of course, with cavalry."

"Shorely; you're safe thar," said Sewall. "Night orders are to reserve fire, unless it's cavalry coming from the enemy's direction. What with the brush and the mix-up, we might shoot into our own men; but not with cavalry patrols. That's safe all around."

The talk ebbed. Luther Jones yawned; he breathed heavily, black beard sweeping his chest. Sewall yawned. Jeff Mindlery found himself nodding. All the outpost sat blinking under their ragged hats; the brush was still and quiet.

Abruptly, the trees rang to a volley. Mindlery leaped up with the others, peering and listening. Musket locks clicked.

"Picket guard," declared Sewall. "They wouldn't fire like that at nothing. Listen!"

Shouts sounded from the left, toward the Turnpike road. Then came the snortings of horses, a crashing amid the brush.

"Cavalry, by Gawd! A Yank patrol!" Jones yawped.

"Headin' this way," added Sewall. "Can you see 'em?"

"Nary a sign; lay low. They got turned. Makin' for the Plank Road—"

More crashes in the brush, a jingling of accouterments. Cavalry, sure enough, at a quick trot.

"I see 'em!" cried Mindlery. His long musket came up.

"Old Jack's orders, boys," said Sewall. "Hold fire till I give word. Then let go."

The shadowy horsemen were obliquing straight toward the squad. They were dimly visible now. Riders, cloaked from neck to heels, ducking the tree-limbs, vague amid the shadows of the pines; then suddenly looming closer, within forty yards.

"Now!" exclaimed Sewall.

Jeff Mindlery felt his musket jar. On either side of him flared the weapons of Sewall and Luther Jones. The outpost's full volley smacked through the woods; it was a surprise to that party of Yankee cavalry, sure enough. The file tossed in a wild upheaval of men and horses. With frantic shouts, a crash and scurry, they vanished as frightened horses took the bits and bolted. Mindlery's ears were still echoing with the volley.

"That fixed 'em!" exclaimed Sewall grimly. "They've skedaddled. Looked like officers, surveying the ground, I reckon. We emptied saddles, I bet; can't tell till morning."

Mindlery was reloading. "I know I emptied one. Wish I hadn't, but I threw up and let go, same as at a coon. All I need is a chance and a good guess. I got one, anyhow."

"Well, don't feel bad about it," said somebody, with a laugh. "We had orders from Old Jack himself, and we obeyed 'em. If we—"

"Look out!" cried Luther Jones. "Down flat! Jump!"

No need of warning. The woods shook, redly illumined by bursting shells. Canister whipped among the trees like driven hail. Mindlery fell flat with the others, groveling, clasping the ground while the iron hissed and spatted above. He heard Sewall's voice.

"That's an answer to us. The cavalry had their look, and a damned Yank battery is posted in the Plank Road to shell us out of here! We'd better get out—"

"The Yanks are charging! Look out!" yelled somebody.

From the direction of the Plank Road to the right, the final burst of artillery merged into the throaty Northern cheer: "Hurray! Hurray!" The brush was all a-crackle; a drum of pounding feet made itself heard.

"Come on!" Sewall rose, and went plunging away at a crouch. Jones ran; Mindlery ran; all of them pelted on together for their own line. Then a new yell checked them: the Southern yell this time. Skirmishers came deployed, running. A crisscross musketry fire filled the air with lead. Sewall dropped again and flattened.

"Wait it out, boys, till we can get clear!"

They hugged the earth again. Suddenly as it came, the skirmish quieted. At Sewall's order, they all rose again and made for the Plank Road. Artillery opened afresh, ceased once more. Then, to Jeff Mindlery and to all of them, came an abrupt and frightful confusion. Yanks appeared, with a rain of bullets. A gray column came boiling along and met the Union force full tilt. Bayonets at work, a mad hurly-burly everywhere.

The Yanks were pressed back; the gray surged on; artillery opened again and shattered them. Ranks hastily formed up, another charge at the Yanks....No go. The artillery broke them. Survivors streamed back through the trees.

The artillery ceased. The silence was sullen and heavy, broken by cries and groans of hurt men. Mindlery and the others of the outpost came into the road at last and paused. A hand litter was coming along, borne at a stagger. A hobbling staff officer halted the bearers briefly and sank down to rest. The outpost crowded around. A sudden cry broke from several men at once. Mindlery saw the whitened features of Stonewall Jackson, the sopping red bandages.

"It's Old Jack!" cried out Sewall in a strangled voice. "The Yanks got him!"

"No," said the staff officer wearily. "We were on reconnoiter. Our own men fired into us."

"What?" gasped Sewall. *"Our* men? It couldn't be—"

"It was. We were on the way in. Outposts took us for Federal cavalry, I guess. One cut us up, over on the Turnpike. We made for the Plank Road through the brush, and another outpost fired before we saw 'em. The General got three bullets—his horse ran off with him, and he fell a piece farther on. We got him under a tree when the battery opened. Both sides charged right over us. We're takin' him back to the hospital."

"He's hit mortal?" quavered Luther Jones.

"Two in the left arm, one through the right hand. The ball through the upper arm cut the artery. Mortal? I dunno. Come on, boys—lift him up."

The officer hobbled on; the white still features of Old Jack disappeared. The outpost squad, in sudden awful comprehension, looked one at another then down at Jeff Mindlery. He had fallen on his knees, both hands clasped to his face, shutting out the world; and horrible dry sobs shook him.

"Oh, Gawd, Gawd!" came his voice, almost past recognition. "Killed my general! Saved my fire, only to kill my general! Oh, I wisht it had been my brother! Might have been anybody else, but it had to be Old Jack! His blood's on my head—"

"Sho', now! For Gawd's sake, stop it!" blurted out Tom Sewall. "Don't take it to yourself, Jeff. It was me give the order. We all of us fired."

Jeff Mindlery's voice broke out again, shrill and spasmodic, a frightful sound.

"My ball—high up at the left shoulder! Might ha' been his heart, but he likely moved. I know where I hold; I took at the first in line. Didn't know it was him. I've killed my general, murdered him—"

"Stop it! My Gawd, will you shet up?" cried Sewall, frantic with horror. "It was orders to shoot. Don't go off your head. We can't help it none."

Mindlery lifted his face, blinked.

"Why was I made to do it? He was my cause; he was everything. He reckoned he was in the right, and so did I. Now I can't name my next young 'un for him. I can't go home to tell about him, when I murdered him. His blood's on me. I can't go home at all, never, never! His blood's on my head—I'm accursed."

"Come on, get out of here," exclaimed Luther Jones. "I can't stand it. Cheer up, Jeff; warn't your fault nohow. It was by his own orders; he knows it was a mistake."

Jeff Mindlery staggered up and groped for his musket. With a sudden step he clubbed the musket and swung it against a tree. The gun broke at the grip; the barrel flew into the brush, and he hurled the stock after the iron. Tears streaming on his cheeks, he shook a fist in the air.

"I killed Old Jack!" came his tragic croak of a voice. "I'll fight no more. I got no place to go now. His blood's on my head. I murdered him, murdered him—and I'd ha' died for him!"

He turned, broke into a blind shambling run, and disappeared quickly among the dark trees.

The other men looked one at another, cursed softly, stood silent. Tom Sewall caught sight of something white on the ground and stooped for it. It was Mindlery's letter home, fallen from his pocket.

"Hey!" exclaimed someone. "He'll be listed as a deserter!"

"It don't matter," said Sewall huskily. "I don't guess anybody will be looking him up anyhow. You boys keep your mouths shut about him. And to think it didn't need to have happened at all—"

He paused, eyeing the letter in his hand.

"What didn't, Tom?" asked a voice.

"Any of it—any of it!" he broke out. "If the Gen'ral had only rid a white horse, it wouldn't have happened. You can 'most always see a white horse at night....Come on, and let's get out of here."

It needn't have happened—and the blue St. Andrew's cross with the white stars, the Southern battle flag that clutched at all hearts, drooped listless like a broken thing before the house where Thomas Jonathan Jackson lay dead upon the wings of victory.

> *Stack arms, men! Come, pile on the rails,*
> *Stir up the campfire bright;*
> *No matter if the canteen fails,*
> *We'll make a roaring night!*
> *Here Shenandoah brawls along,*
> *There burly Blue Ridge echoes strong,*
> *To swell the brigade's rousing song*
> *Of Stonewall Jackson's way!*

Gettysburg

Mary Johnston

The sun of the first day of July rose serene into an azure sky where a few white clouds were floating. The light summer mist was dissipated; a morning wind, freshly sweet, rippled the corn and murmured in the green and lusty trees. The sunshine gilded Little Round Top and Big Round Top, gilded Culp"s Hill and Cemetery Hill, gilded Oak Hill and Seminary Ridge. It flashed from the cupola of the Pennsylvania College. McPherson"s Woods caught it on its topmost branches, and the trees of Peach Orchard. It trembled between the leaves, and flecked with golden petals Menchey"s Spring and Spangler"s Spring. It lay in sleepy lengths on the Emmitsburg Road. It struck the boulders of the Devil"s Den; it made indescribably light and fine the shocked wheat in a wheat-field that drove into the green like a triangular golden wedge. Full in the centre of the rich landscape it made a shining mark, a golden bull"s-eye, of the small town of Gettysburg.

It should have been all peace, that rich Pennsylvania landscape—a Dutch peace—a Quaker peace. Market wains and country folk should have moved upon the roads, and a boy, squirrel-hunting, should have been the most murderous thing in the Devil"s Den. Corn-blades should have glistened, not bayonets; for the fluttering flags the farmers" wives should have been bleaching linen on the grass; for marching feet there should have risen the sound of the scythe in the wheat; for the groan of gun-wheels upon the roads the robin"s song and the bob white"s call.

The sun mounted. He was well above the tree-tops when the first shot was fired—Heth"s brigade of A.P. Hill"s corps encountering Buford"s cavalry.

The sun went down the first day red behind the hills. He visited the islands of the Pacific, Nippon, and the Kingdom of Flowers, and India and Iran. He crowned Caucasus with gold, and showered largess over Europe. He reddened the waves of the Atlantic. He touched with his spear lighthouses and coast towns and the inland green land. He came up over torn orchard and trampled wheat-field; he came up over the Round Tops and Culp"s Hill and Cemetery Hill. But no one, this second day, stopped to watch his rising. The battle-smoke hid him from the living upon the slopes and in all the fields.

The sun traveled from east to west, but no man on the shield of which Gettysburg was the boss saw him go down that second day. A thick smoke, like the wings of countless ravens, kept out the parting gleams. He went his way over the plains of the west and the Pacific and the Asian lands. He came over Europe and the Atlantic and made, on the third morning, bright pearl of the lighthouses, the surf, and the shore. The ripe July country welcomed him. But around Gettysburg his rising was not seen. The smoke had not dispersed. He rode on high, but all that third day he was seen far away and dim as through crêpe. All day he shone serene on other lands, but above this region he hung small and dim and remote like a tarnished, antique shield. Sometimes the drift of ravens" wings hid him quite. An incense mounted to him, a dark smell and a dark vapor.

The birds were gone from the trees, the cattle from the fields, the children from the lanes and the brookside. All left on the first day. There was a hollow between Round Top and Devil"s Den, and into this the anxious farmers had driven and penned a herd of cattle. On the sunny, calm afternoon when they had done this they could not conceive that any battle would affect this hollow. Here the oxen, the cows, would be safe from chance bullet and from forager. But the farmers did not guess the might of that battle.

The stream of shells was directed against Round Top, but a number, black and heavy, rained into the hollow. A great milk-white ox was the first wounded. He lay with his side ripped open, a ghastly sight. Then a cow with calf was mangled, then a young steer had both fore-legs broken. Bellowing, the maddened herd rushed here and there, attacking the rough sides of the hollow. Death and panic were upon the slopes as well as at the bottom of the basin. A bursting shell killed and wounded a dozen at once. The air grew thick and black, and filled with the cries of these brutes.

A courier, returning to his general after delivering an order, had his horse shot beneath him. Disentangling himself, he went on, on foot, through a wood. He was intolerably thirsty—and lo, a spring! It was small and round and clear like a mirror, and as he knelt he saw his own face and thought, "She wouldn"t know me." The minies were so continuously singing that he had ceased to heed them. He drank, then saw that he was reddening the water. He did not know when he had been wounded, but now, as he tried to rise, he grew so faint and cold that he knew that Death had met him.—There was moss and fern and a nodding white flower. It was not a bad place in which to die. In a pocket within his gray jacket he had a daguerreotype—a young and smiling face and form. His fingers were so nerveless now that it was hard to get the little velvet case out, and when it was out, it proved to be shattered, it and the picture within. The smiling face and form were all marred, unrecognizable. So small a thing, perhaps!—but it made the bitterness of this soldier"s death. The splintered case in his hands, he died as goes to sleep a child who has been unjustly punished. His body sank deep among the fern, his chest heaved, he shook his head faintly, and then it dropped upon the moss, between the stems of the nodding white flower.

A long Confederate line left a hillside and crossed an open space of corn-field and orchard. Double quick it moved, under its banners, under the shells shrieking above. The guns changed range, and an iron flail struck the line. It wavered, wavered. A Federal line leaped a stone wall, and swept forward, under its banners, hurrahing. Midway of the wide open there was stretched beneath the murky sky a narrow web—woof of gray, warp of blue. The strip held while the heart beat a minute or more, then it parted. The blue edge went backward over the plain; the gray edge, after a moment, rushed after. *"Yaaaiihhh! Yaaaiiihhhh!"* it yelled,—and its red war-flag glowed like fire. The gray commander-in-chief watched from a hillside, a steady light in his eyes. Over against him on another hill, Meade, the blue general, likewise watched. To the South, across the distant Potomac, lay the vast, beleaguered Southern fortress. Its gate had opened; out had poured a vast sally party, a third of its bravest and best, and at the head the leader most trusted, most idolized. Out had rushed the Army of Northern Virginia. It had crossed the moat of the Potomac; it was here, on the beleaguer"s ground.

Earth and heaven were shaking with the clangor of two shields. The sky was whirring and dim, but there might be imagined, suspended there, a huge balance—here the besiegers, here the fortress"s best and bravest. Which would this day, or these days, tip the beam? Much hung upon that—all might be said to hang upon that. The waves on the plain rolled forward, rolled back, rolled forward. When the sun went down the first day the fortress"s battle-flag was in the ascendant.

A great red barn was the headquarters of "dear Dick Ewell." He rode with Gordon and others at a gallop down a smoky road between stone fences. "Wish Old Jackson was here!" he said. "Wish Marse Robert had Old Jackson! This is the watershed, General Gordon—yes, sir! this is the watershed of the War! If it doesn"t still go right to-day—It seems to me that wall there"s got a suspicious look—"

The wall in question promptly justified the suspicion. There came from behind it a volley that emptied gray saddles. Gordon heard the thud of the minie as it struck Old Dick. "Are you hurt, sir? Are you hurt?"

"No, no, General! I"m not hurt. But if that ball had struck you, sir, we"d have had the trouble of carrying you off the field. I"m a whole lot better fixed than you for a fight! It don"t hurt a mite to be shot in a wooden leg."

Three gray soldiers lay behind a shock of wheat. They were young men, old school-mates. This wheat-shock marked the farthest point attained in a desperate charge made by their regiment against a larger force. It was one of those charges in which everybody sees that if a miracle happens it will be all right, and that if it doesn"t happen—It was one of those charges in which first an officer stands out, waving his sword, then a man or two follow him, then three or four more, then all waver back, only to start forth again, then others join, then the officer cries aloud, then, with a roar, the line springs forward and rushes over the field, in the cannon"s mouth. Such had been the procedure in this charge. The miracle had not happened.—After a period of mere din as of ocean waves the three found themselves behind this heap of tarnished gold. When, gasping, they looked round, all their fellows had gone back; they saw them, a distant torn line, still holding the flag. Then a rack of smoke came between, hiding flag and all. The three seemed alone in the world. The wheat-ears made a low inner sound like reeds in quiet marshes. The smoke lifted just enough to let a muddy sunlight touch an acre of the dead.

"We"ve got," said one of the young men, "to get out of here. They"ll be counter-charging in a minute."

"O God! let them charge."

"Harry, are you afraid—"

"Yes; I"m afraid—sick and afraid. O God, O God!"

The oldest of the three, moving his head very cautiously, looked round the wheat-shock. "The Army of the Potomac"s coming." He rose to his knees, facing the other way. "It"s two hundred yards to the regiment. Well, we always won the races at the old Academy. I"ll start, Tom, and then you follow, and then you, Harry, you come straight along!"

He rose to his feet, took the posture of a runner, drew a deep breath and started. Two yards from the shock a cannon ball sheared the head from the body. The body fell, jetting blood. The head bounded back within the shadow of the wheat-shock. Tom was already standing, bent like a bow. A curious sound came from his lips, he glanced aside, then ran. He ran as swiftly as an Indian, swiftly and well. The minie did not find him until he was half-way across the field. Then it did, and he threw up his arms and fell. Harry, on his hands and knees, turned from side to side an old, old face, bloodless and twisted. He heard the Army of the Potomac coming, and in front lay the corpses. He tried to get to his feet, but his joints were water, and there was a crowd of black atoms before his eyes. A sickness, a clamminess, a despair—and all in eternities. Then the sound swelled, and drove him as the cry of the hounds the hare. He ran, panting, but the charge now swallowed up the wheat-shock and came thundering on. In front were only the dead, piled at the foot of the wall of smoke. He still clutched his gun, and now, with a shrill cry, he stopped, turned, and stood at bay. He had hurt a hunter in the leg, before the blue muskets clubbed him down.

A regiment, after advancing a skirmish line, moved over broken and boulder-strewn ground to occupy a yet defended position. In front moved the colonel, half-turned toward his men, encouraging them in a rich and hearty voice. "Come on, men! Come on, come on! You are all good harvesters, and the grain is ripe, the grain is ripe! Come on, every mother"s son of you! Run now! just as though there were home and children up there! Come on! Come on!"

The regiment reached a line of flat boulders. There was a large flat one like an altar slab, that the colonel must spring upon and cross. Upon it, outstretched, face upward, in a pool of blood, lay a young figure, a lieutenant of skirmishers, killed a quarter of an hour ago. "Come on! Come on!" shouted the colonel, his face turned to his men. "Victory! To-night we"ll write home about the victory!"

His foot felt for the top edge of the boulder. He sprang upon it, and faced with suddenness the young dead. The oncoming line saw him stand as if frozen, then with a stiff jerk up went the sword again. "Come on! Come on!" he cried, and plunging from the boulder continued to mount the desired slope. His men, close behind him, also encountered the dead on the altar slab. "Good God! It"s Lieutenant—It"s his son!" But in front the colonel"s changed voice continued its crying: "Come on! Come on! Come on!"

A stone wall, held by the gray, leaped fire, rattled and smoked. It did this at short intervals for a long while, a brigade of the enemy choosing to charge at like intervals. The gray"s question was a question of ammunition. So long as the ammunition held out, so would they and the wall. They sent out foragers for cartridges. Four men having secured a quantity from an impatiently sympathetic reserve, heaped them in a blanket, made a large bundle, and slung it midway of a musket. One man took the butt, another the muzzle, and as they had to reckon with sharp-shooters going back, the remaining two marched in front. All double-quicked where the exposure was not extreme, and ran where it was. The echoing goal grew larger—as did also a clump of elms at right angles with the wall. Vanguard cocked his eye. "Buzzards in those trees, boys—blue buzzards!"

Vanguard pitched forward as he spoke. The three ran on. Ten yards, and the man who had been second and was now first, was picked off. The two ran on, the cartridges between them. "We"re goners!" said the one, and the other nodded as he ran.

There was a gray battery somewhere in the smoke, and now by chance or intention it flung into the air a shell that shrieked its way straight to the clump of elms, and exploded in the round of leaf and branch. The sharp-shooters were stilled. "Moses and the prophets!" said the runners. "That"s a last year"s bird"s nest!"

Altogether the foragers brought in ammunition enough to serve the gray wall"s immediate purpose. It cracked and flamed for another while, and then the blue brigade ceased its charges and went elsewhere. It went thinned—oh, thinned!—in numbers. The gray waited a little for the smoke to lift, and then it mounted the wall. "And the ground before us," says a survivor, "was the most heavenly blue!"

A battalion of artillery, thundering across a corner of the field, went into position upon a little hill-top. Facing it was Cemetery Hill and a tall and wide-arched gateway. This gateway, now clearly seen, now withdrawn behind a world of gray smoke, now showing a half arch, an angle, a span of the crest, exercised a fascination. The gunners, waiting for the word, watched it. "Gate of Death, don"t it look?—Gate of Death."—"Wonder what"s beyond?—Yankees."—"But they ain"t dead—they"re alive and kicking."—"Now it"s hidden—Gate of Death."—"This battle"s going to lay over Sharps-burg—Over Gaines"s Mill—Over Malvern Hill—Over Fredericksburg—Over Second Manassas—Over"—"The—Gate"s hidden—There"s a battery over there going to open"—"One? There"s two, there"s three—" *Cannoneers to your pieces!*

A shell dug into the earth and exploded. There was a heavy rain of dark earth. It pattered against all the pieces. It showered men and horses, and for a minute made a thick twilight of the air. "Whew! the Earth"s taking a hand! Anybody hurt?" *Howitzer, load!*

"Gate of Death"s clear."

An artillery lieutenant—Robert Stiles—acting as volunteer aide to Gordon, was to make his way across the battlefield with information for Edward Johnson. The ground was strewn with the dead, the air was a shrieking torrent of shot and shell. The aide and his horse thought only of the thing in hand—getting across that field, getting across with the order. The aide bent to the horse"s neck; the horse laid himself to the ground and raced like a wild horse before a prairie fire. The aide thought of nothing; he was going to get the order there; for the rest his mind seemed as useless as a mirror with a curtain before it. Afterwards, however, when he had time to look he found in the mirror pictures enough. Among them was a picture of a battalion—Latimer"s battalion. "Never, before or after, did I see fifteen or twenty guns in such a condition of wreck and destruction as this battalion was! It had been hurled backward as it were by the very weight and impact of metal from the position it had occupied on the crest of a little ridge, into a saucer-shaped depression behind it; and such a scene as it presented—guns dismounted and disabled, carriages splintered and crushed, ammunition chests exploded, limbers upset, wounded horses plunging and kicking, dashing out the brains of men tangled in the harness; while cannoneers with pistols were crawling round through the wreck shooting the struggling horses to save the lives of the wounded men."

Hood and his Texans and Law"s Alabamians were trying to take Little Round Top. They drove out the line of sharpshooters behind the stone wall girdling the height. Back went the blue, up the steeps, up to their second line, behind a long ledge of rock. Up and after went the gray. The tall boulders split the advance like the teeth of a comb; no alignment could be kept. The rocks formed defiles where only two or three could go abreast. The way was steep and horrible, and from above rained the bullets. Up went the gray, reinforced now by troops from McLaws" division; up they went and took the second line. Back and up went the blue to the bald and rocky crest, to their third line, a stronghold, indeed, and strongly held. Up and on came the gray, but it was as though the sky were raining lead. The gray fell like leaves in November when the winds howl around Round Top. Oh, the boulders! The blood on the boulders, making them slippery! Oh, the torn limbs of trees, falling so fast! The eyes smarted in the smoke; the voice choked in the throat. All men were hoarse with shouting.

Darkness and light went in flashes, but the battle-odor stayed, and the unutterable volume of sound. All the dogs of war were baying. The muscles strained, the foot mounted. Forward and up went the battle-flag, red ground and blue cross. Now the boulders were foes, and now they were shields. Men knelt behind them and fired upward. Officers laid aside their swords, took the muskets from the dead, knelt and fired. But the crest of Round Top darted lightnings—lightnings and bolts of leaden death. Death rained from Round Top, and the drops beat down the gray. Hood was badly hurt in the arm. Pender fell mortally wounded. Anderson was wounded. Semmes fell mortally hurt. Barksdale received here his death-wound. Amid the howl of the storm, in the leaden air, in scorching, in blood and pain and tumult and shouting, the small, unheeded disk of the sun touched the western rim of the earth.

A wounded man lay all night in Devil"s Den. There were other wounded there, but the great boulders hid them from one another. This man lay in a rocky angle, upon the over-hanging lip of the place. Below him, smoke clung like a cerement to the far-flung earth. For a time smoke was about him, thick in his nostrils. For a time it hid the sky. But now all firing was stayed, the night was wheeling on, and the smoke lifted. Below, vague in the night-time, were seen flickering lights—torches, he knew, ambulances, litter-bearers, lifting, serving one in a hundred. They were far-away, scattered over the stricken field. They would not come up here to Devil"s Den. He knew they would not come, and he watched them as the shipwrecked watch the sail upon the horizon that has not seen their signal, and that will not see it. He, shipwrecked here, had waved no cloth, but, idle as it was, he had tried to shout. His voice had fallen like a broken-winged bird. Now he lay, in a pool of his own blood, not greatly in pain, but dying. Presently he grew light-headed, though not so much so but that he knew that he was light-headed, and could from time to time reason with his condition. He was a reading man, and something of a thinker, and now his mind in its wanderings struck into all manner of by-paths.

For a time he thought that the field below was the field of Waterloo. He remembered seeing, while it was yet light, a farm-house, a distant cluster of buildings with a frightened air. "La Belle Alliance," he thought, "or Hougoumont—which?—These Belgians planted a lot of wheat, and now there are red poppies all through it.—Where is Ney and his cavalry?—No, Stuart and his cavalry—" His mind righted for a moment. "This is a long battle, and a long night. Come, Death! Come, Death!" The shadowy line of boulders became a line of Deaths, tall, draped figures bearing scythes. Three Deaths, then a giant hour-glass, then three Deaths, then the hour-glass. He stared, fascinated. "Which scythe? The one that starts out of line—now if I can keep them still in line—just so long will I live!" He stared for a while, till the Deaths became boulders again and his fingers fell to playing with the thickening blood on the ground beside him. A meteor pierced the night—a white fire-ball thrown from the ramparts of the sky. He seemed to be rushing with it, rushing, rushing, rushing,—a rushing river. There was a heavy sound. A clear voice said in his ear, "That was the last grain of sand in the hour-glass." As his head sank back he saw again the line of Deaths, and the one that left the line.

Below, through the night, the wind that blew over the wheat-fields and the meadows, the orchards and the woods, was a moaning wind. It was a wind with a human voice.

Dawn came, but the guns smeared her translucence with black. The sun rose, but the ravens" wings hid him. Dull-red and sickly-copper was this day, hidden and smothered by dark wreaths. Many things happened in it; variation and change that cast a tendril toward the future.

Day drove on; sultry and loud and smoky. A squad of soldiers in a fence-corner, waiting for the order forward, exchanged opinions. "Three days. We"re going to fight forever—and ever—and ever."—"You may be. I ain"t. I"m going to fight through to where there"s peace—" ""Peace!" How do you spell it?"—""They cry Peace! Peace! and there is no Peace!"" —"D"ye reckon if one of us took a bucket and went over to that spring there, he"d be shot?"—"Of course he would! Besides, where"s the bucket?"—"I"ve got a canteen"—"I"ve got a cup"—"Say, Sergeant, can we go?"—"No. You"ll be killed."—"I"d just as soon be killed as die of thirst! Besides a shell"ll come plumping down directly and kill us anyhow—" "Talk of something pleasant."—"Jim"s caught a grasshopper! Poor little hoppergrass, you oughtn"t to be out here in this wide and wicked world! Let him go, Jim."—"How many killed and wounded do you reckon there are?"—"Thirty thousand of us, and sixty thousand of them."—"I wish that smoke would lift so"s we could see something!"—*Look out! Look out! Get out of this!*

Two men crawled away from the crater made by the shell. A heavy tussock of grass in their path stopped them. One rose to his knees, the other, who was wounded, took the posture of the dying Gaul in the Capitoline. "Who are you?" said the one. "I am Jim Dudley. Who are you?"—"I—I didn"t know you, Jim. I"m Randolph.—Well, we"re all that"s left."

The dead horses lay upon this field one and two and three days in the furnace heat. They were fearful to see and there came from them a fetid odor. But the scream of the wounded horses was worse than the sight of the dead. There were many wounded horses. They lay in wood and field, in country lane and orchard. No man tended them, and they knew not what it was all about. To and fro and from side to side of the vast, cloud-wreathed Mars" Shield galloped the riderless horses.

At one of the clock all the guns, blue and gray, opened in a cannonade that shook the leaves of distant trees. A smoke as of Vesuvius or Etna, sulphurous, pungent, clothed the region of battle. The air reverberated and the hills trembled. The roar was like the roar of the greatest cataract of a larger world, like the voice of a storm sent by the King of all the Genii. Amid its deep utterance the shout even of many men could not be heard.

Out from the ranks of the fortress"s defenders rushed a gray, world-famous charge. It was a division charging—three brigades *en échelon*—five thousand men, led by a man with long auburn locks. Down a hill, across a rolling open, up an opposite slope,—half a mile in all, perhaps,—lay their road. Mars and Bellona may be figured in the air above it. It was a spectacle, that charge, fit to draw the fierce eyes and warm the gloomy souls of all the warrior deities. Woden may have watched and the Aztec god. The blue artillery crowned that opposite slope, and other slopes. The blue artillery swung every muzzle; it spat death upon the five thousand. The five thousand went steadily, gray, and cool, and clear, the vivid flag above them. A light was on their bayonets—the three lines of bayonets—the three brigades. Garnett and Kemper and Armistead. A light was in the eyes of the men; they saw the fortress above the battle-clouds; they saw their homes, and the watchers upon the ramparts. They went steadily, to the eyes of history in a curious, unearthly light, the light of a turn in human affairs, the light of catastrophe, the light of an ending and a beginning.

When they came into the open between the two heights, the massed blue infantry turned every rifle against them. There poured a leaden rain of death. Here, too, the three lines met an enfilading fire from the batteries on Round Top. Death howled and threw himself against the five thousand; in the air above might be heard the Valkyries calling. There were not now five thousand, there were not now four thousand. There was a clump of trees seen like spectres through the smoke. It rose from the slope which was the gray goal, from the slope peopled by Federal batteries, with a great Federal infantry support at hand. Toward this slope, up this slope went Pickett"s Charge.

Garnett fell dead. Kemper and Trimble were desperately wounded. Save Pickett himself all mounted officers were down. The men fell—the men fell; Death swung a fearful scythe. There were not now four thousand; there were not now three thousand. And still the vivid flag went on; and still, *"Yaaaaih! Yaaaaiihhhh! Yaiiihhhaaiihhh!"* yelled Pickett"s Charge.

There was a stone wall to cross. Armistead, his hat on the point of his waved sword, leaped upon the coping. A bullet pierced his breast; he fell and died. By now, by now the charge was whittled thin! Oh, thick as the leaves of Vallombrosa the fortress"s dearest and best lay upon that slope beneath the ravens" wings! On went the thin, fierce ranks, on and over the wall, on and up, into the midst of the enemy"s guns. The two flags strained toward each other; the hands of the gray were upon the guns of the blue; there came a wild mêlée.—There were not two thousand now, and the guns were yet roaring, and the blue infantry gathered from all sides—

"The smoke," says one Luther Hopkins, a gray soldier who was at Gettysburg, "the smoke rose higher and higher and spread wider and wider, hiding the sun, and then, gently dropping back, hid from human eyes the dreadful tragedy. But the battle went on and on, and the roar of the guns continued. After a while, when the sun was sinking to rest, there was a hush. The noise died away. The winds came creeping back from the west, and gently lifting the coverlet of smoke, revealed a strange sight. The fields were all carpeted, a beautiful carpet, a costly carpet, more costly than Axminster or velvet. The figures were horses and men all matted and woven together with skeins of scarlet thread."

Chickamauga

Thomas Wolfe

On the seventh day of August, 1861, I was nineteen years of age. If I live to the seventh day of August this year I'll be ninety-five years old. And the way I feel this mornin' I intend to live. Now I guess you'll have to admit that that's goin' a good ways back.

I was born up at the Forks of the Toe River in 1842. Your grandpaw, boy, was born at the same place in 1828. His father, and mine, too, Bill Pentland—your great-grandfather, boy—moved into that region way back right after the Revolutionary War and settled at the Forks of Toe. The real Indian name fer hit was Estatoe, but the white men shortened hit to Toe, and hit's been known as Toe River ever since.

Of course hit was all Indian country in those days. I've heared that the Cherokees helped Bill Pentland's father build the first house he lived in, where some of us was born. I've heared, too, that Bill Pentland's grandfather came from Scotland back before the Revolution, and that thar was three brothers. That's all the Pentlands that I ever heared of in this country. If you ever meet a Pentland anywheres you can rest assured he's descended from one of those three.

Well, now, as I was tellin' you, upon the seventh day of August, 1861, I was nineteen years of age. At seven-thirty in the mornin' of that day I started out from home and walked the whole way in to Clingman. Jim Weaver had come over from Big Hickory where he lived the night before and stayed with me. And now he went along with me. He was the best friend I had. We had growed up alongside of each other: now we was to march alongside of each other fer many a long and weary mile—how many neither of us knowed that mornin' when we started out.

Hit was a good twenty mile away from where we lived to Clingman, and I reckon young folks nowadays would consider twenty mile a right smart walk. But fer people in those days hit wasn't anything at all. All of us was good walkers. Why Jim Weaver could keep goin' without stoppin' all day long.

Jim was big and I was little, about the way you see me now, except that I've shrunk up a bit, but I could keep up with him anywhere he went. We made hit into Clingman before twelve o'clock—hit was a hot day, too—and by three o'clock that afternoon we had both joined up with the Twenty-ninth. That was my regiment from then on, right on to the end of the war. Anyways, I was an enlisted man that night, the day that I was nineteen years of age, and I didn't see my home again fer four long years.

Your Uncle Bacchus, boy, was already in Virginny: we knowed he was thar because we'd had a letter from him. He joined up right at the start with the Fourteenth. He'd already been at First Manassas and I reckon from then on he didn't miss a big fight in Virginny fer the next four years, except after Antietam he got wounded and was laid up fer four months.

Even way back on those days your Uncle Bacchus had those queer religious notions that you've heard about. The Pentlands are good people, but everyone who ever knowed 'em knows they can go queer on religion now and then. That's the reputation that they've always had. And that's the way Back was. He was a Russellite even in those days: accordin' to his notions the world was comin' to an end and he was goin' to be right in on hit when hit happened. That was the way he had hit figgered out. He was always prophesyin' and predictin' even back before the war, and when the war came, why Back just knowed that this was hit.

Why law! He wouldn't have missed that war fer any-thing. Back didn't go to war because he wanted to kill

Yankees. He didn't want to kill nobody. He was as tender-hearted as a baby and as brave as a lion. Some fellers told hit on him later how they'd come on him at Gettysburg, shootin' over a stone wall, and his rifle bar'l had got so hot he had to put hit down and rub his hands on the seat of his pants because they got so blistered. He was singin' hymns, they said, with tears a-streamin' down his face—that's the way they told hit, anyway—and every time he fired he'd sing another verse. And I reckon he killed plenty because when Back had a rifle in his hands he didn't miss.

But he was a good man. He didn't want to hurt a fly. And I reckon the reason that he went to war was because he thought he'd be at Armageddon. That's the way he had hit figgered out, you know. When the war came, Back said: "Well, this is hit, and I'm a-goin' to be thar. The hour has come," he said, "when the Lord is goin' to set up His Kingdom here on earth and separate the sheep upon the right hand and the goats upon the left—jest like hit was predicted long ago—and I'm a-goin' to be thar when hit happens."

Well, we didn't ask him which side *he* was goin' to be on, but we all knowed which side without havin' to ask. Back was goin' to be on the *sheep* side—that's the way *he* had hit figgered out. And that's the way he had hit figgered out right up to the day of his death ten years ago. He kept prophesyin' and predictin' right up to the end. No matter what happened, no matter what mistakes he made, he kept right on predictin'. First he said the war was goin' to be the Armageddon day. And when that didn't happen he said hit was goin' to come along in the eighties. And when hit didn't happen then he moved hit up to the nineties. And when the war broke out in 1914 and the whole world had to go, why Bacchus knowed that that was hit.

And no matter how hit all turned out, Back never would give in or own up he was wrong. He'd say he'd made a mistake in his figgers somers, but that he'd found out what hit was and that next time he'd be right. And that's the way he was up to the time he died.

I had to laugh when I heared the news of his death, because of course, accordin' to Back's belief, after you die nothin' happens to you fer a thousand years. You jest lay in your grave and sleep until Christ comes and wakes you up.

So that's why I had to laugh. I'd a-give anything to've been there the next mornin' when Back woke up and found himself in heaven. I'd've give any thing just to've seen the expression on his face. I may have to wait a bit but I'm goin' to have some fun with him when I see him. But I'll bet you even then he won't give in. He'll have some reason fer hit, he'll try to argue he was right but that he made a little mistake about hit somers in his figgers.

But Back was a good man—a better man than Bacchus Pentland never lived. His only failin' was the failin' that so many Pentlands have—he went and got queer religious notions and he wouldn't give them up.

Well, like I say then, Back was in the Fourteenth. Your Uncle Sam and Uncle George was with the Seventeenth, and all three of them was in Lee's army in Virginny. I never seed nor heared from either Back or Sam fer the next four years. I never knowed what had happened to them or whether they was dead or livin' until I got back home in '65. And of course I never heared from George again until they wrote me after Chancellorsville. And then I knowed that he was dead. They told hit later when I came back home that hit took seven men to take him. They asked him to surrender. And then they had to kill him because he wouldn't be taken. That's the way he was. He never would give up. When they got to his dead body they told how they had to crawl over a whole heap of dead Yankees before they found him. And then they knowed hit was George. That's the way he was, all right. He never would give in.

He is buried in the Confederate cemetery at Richmond, Virginny. Bacchus went through thar more than twenty years ago on his way to the big reunion up at Gettysburg. He hunted up his grave and found out where he was.

That's where Jim and me thought that we'd be too. I mean with Lee's men, in Virginny. That's where we thought that we was goin' when we joined. But, like I'm goin' to tell you now, hit turned out different from the way we thought.

Bob Saunders was our Captain; L.C. McIntyre our Major; and Leander Briggs the Colonel of our regiment. They kept us thar at Clingman fer two weeks. Then they marched us into Altamont and drilled us fer the next two months. Our drillin' ground was right up and down where Parker Street now is. In those days thar was nothing thar but open fields.

Hit's all built up now. To look at hit today you'd never know thar'd ever been an open field thar. But that's where hit was, all right.

Late in October we was ready and they moved us on. The day they marched us out, Martha Patton came in all the way from Zebulon to see Jim Weaver before we went away. He'd known her fer jest two months; he'd met her the very week we joined up and I was with him when he met her. She came from out along Cane River. Thar was a camp revival meetin' goin' on outside of Clingman at the time, and she was visitin' this other gal in Clingman while the revival lasted; and that was how Jim Weaver met her. We was walkin' along one evenin' toward sunset and we passed this house where she was stayin' with this other gal. And both of them was settin' on the porch as we went past. The other gal was fair, and she was dark: she had black hair and eyes, and she was plump and sort of little, and she had the pertiest complexion, and the pertiest white skin and teeth you ever seed; and when she smiled there was a dimple in her cheeks.

Well, neither of us knowed these gals, and so we couldn't stop and talk to them, but when Jim saw the little 'un he stopped short in his tracks like he was shot, and then looked at her so hard she had to turn her face. Well, then, we walked on down the road a piece and Jim stopped and turned and looked again, and when he did, why, sure enough, he caught her lookin' at him too. And then her face got red—she looked away again.

Well, that was where she landed him. He didn't say a word, but Lord! I felt him jerk there like a trout upon the line—and I knowed right then and thar she had him hooked. We turned and walked on down the road a ways, and then he stopped and looked at me and said:

"Did you see that gal back thar?"

"Do you mean the light one or the dark one?"

"You know damn good and well which one I mean," said Jim.

"Yes, I seed her—what about her?" I said.

"Well, nothin'—only I'm a-goin' to marry her," he said.

I knowed then that she had him hooked. And yet I never believed at first that hit would last. Fer Jim had had so many gals—I'd never had a gal in my whole life up to that time, but Lord! Jim would have him a new gal every other week.

We had some fine-lookin' fellers in our company, but Jim Weaver was the handsomest feller that you ever seed. He was tall and lean and built just right, and he carried himself as straight as a rod: he had black hair and coal-black eyes, and when he looked at you he could burn a hole through you. And I reckon he'd burned a hole right through the heart of many a gal before he first saw Martha Patton. He could have had his pick of the whole lot—a born lady-killer if you ever seed one—and that was why I never thought that hit'd last.

And maybe hit was a pity that hit did. Fer Jim Weaver until the day that he met Martha Patton had been the most happy-go-lucky feller that you ever seed. He didn't have a care in the whole world—full of fun—ready fer anything and into every kind of devilment and foolishness. But from that moment on he was a different man. And I've always thought that maybe hit was a pity that hit hit him when hit did—that hit had to come jest at that time. If hit had only come a few years later—if hit could only have waited till the war was over! He'd wanted to go so much—he'd looked at the whole thing as a big lark—but now! Well she had him, and he had her: the day they marched us out of town he had her promise, and in his watch he had her picture and a little lock of her black hair, and as they marched us out, and him beside me, we passed her, and she looked at him, and I felt him jerk again and knowed the look she gave him had gone through him like a knife.

From that time on he was a different man; from that time on he was like a man in hell. Hit's funny how hit all turns out—how none of hit is like what we expect. Hit's funny how war and a little black-haired gal will change a man—but that's the story that I'm goin' to tell you now.

The nearest rail head in those days was eighty mile away at Locust Gap. They marched us out of town right up the Fairfield Road along the river up past Crestville, and right across the Blue Ridge there, and down the mountain. We made Old Stockade the first day's march and camped thar fer the night. Hit was twenty-four miles of marchin' right across the mountain, with the roads the way they was in those days, too. And let me tell you, fer new men with only two months' trainin' that was doin' good.

We made Locust Gap in three days and a half, and I wish you'd seed the welcome that they gave us! People were hollerin' and shoutin' the whole way. All the women folk and childern were lined up along the road, bands a-playin', boys runnin' along beside us, good shoes, new uniforms, the finest-lookin' set of fellers that you ever seed—Lord! You'd a-thought we was goin' to a picnic from the way hit looked. And I reckon that was the way most of us felt about hit, too. We thought we was goin' off to have a lot of fun. If anyone had knowed what he was in fer or could a-seed the passel o' scarecrows that came limpin' back barefoot and half naked four years later, I reckon he'd a-thought twice before he 'listed up.

Lord, when I think of hit! When I try to tell about hit thar jest ain't words enough to tell what hit was like. And when I think of the way I was when I joined up—and the way I was when I came back four years later! When I went away I was an ignorant country boy, so tender-hearted that I wouldn't harm a rabbit. And when I came back after the war was over I could a-stood by and seed a man murdered right before my eyes with no more feelin' than I'd have had fer a stuck hog. I had no more feelin' about human life than I had fer the life of a sparrer. I'd seed a ten-acre field so thick with dead men that you could have walked all over hit without steppin' on the ground a single time.

And that was where I made my big mistake. If I'd only knowed a little more, if I'd only waited jest a little longer after I got home, things would have been all right. That's been the big regret of my whole life. I never had no education, I never had a chance to git one before I went away. And when I came back I could a-had my schoolin' but I didn't take hit. The reason was I never knowed no better: I'd seed so much fightin' and killin' that I didn't care fer nothin'. I jest felt dead and numb like all the brains had been shot out of me. I jest wanted to git me a little patch of land somewheres and settle down and fergit about the world.

That's where I made my big mistake. I didn't wait long enough. I got married too soon, and after that the childern came and hit was root, hawg, or die: I had to grub fer hit. But if I'd only waited jest a little while hit would have been all right. In less'n a year hit all cleared up. I got my health back, pulled myself together and got my feet back on the ground, and had more mercy and understandin' in me, jest on account of all the sufferin' I'd seen, than I ever had. And as fer my head, why hit was better than hit ever was: with all I'd seen and knowed I could a-got a schoolin' in no time. But you see I wouldn't wait. I didn't think that hit'd ever come back. I was jest sick of livin'.

But as I say—they marched us down to Locust Gap in less'n four days' time, and then they put us on the cars fer Richmond. We got to Richmond on the mornin' of one day, and up to that very moment we had thought that they was sendin' us to join Lee's army in the north. But the next mornin' we got our orders—and they was sendin' us out west. They had been fightin' in Kentucky: we was in trouble thar; they sent us out to stop the Army of the Cumberland. And that was the last I ever saw of old Virginny. From that time on we fought it out thar in the west and south. That's where we war, the Twenty-ninth, from then on to the end.

We had no real big fights until the spring of '62. And hit takes a fight to make a soldier of a man. Before that, thar was skirmishin' and raids in Tennessee and in Kentucky. That winter we seed hard marchin' in the cold and wind and rain. We learned to know what hunger was, and what hit was to have to draw your belly in to fit your rations. I reckon by that time we knowed hit wasn't goin' to be a picnic like we thought that hit would be. We was a-learnin' all the time, but we wasn't soldiers yet. It takes a good big fight to make a soldier, and we hadn't had one yet. Early in '62 we almost had one. They marched us to the relief of Donelson—but law! They had taken her before we got thar—and I'm goin' to tell you a good story about that.

U.S. Grant was thar to take her, and we was marchin' to relieve her before old Butcher could git in. We was seven mile away, and hit was comin' on to sundown—we'd been marchin' hard. We got the order to fall out and rest. And that was when I heared the gun and knowed that Donelson had fallen. Thar was no sound of fightin'. Everything was still as Sunday. We was sittin' thar aside the road and then I heared a cannon boom. Hit boomed five times, real slow like—Boom!—Boom!—Boom!—Boom!—Boom! And the moment that I heared hit, I had a premonition. I turned to Jim and I said: "Well, thar you are! That's Donelson—and she's surrendered!"

Cap'n Bob Saunders heared me, but he wouldn't believe me and he said: "You're wrong!"

"Well," said Jim, "I hope to God he's right. I wouldn't care if the whole damn war had fallen through. I'm ready to go home."

"Well, he's wrong," said Captain Bob, "and I'll bet money on hit that he is."

Well, I tell you, that jest suited me. That was the way I was in those days—right from the beginnin' of the war to the very end. If thar was any fun or devilment goin' on, any card playin' or gamblin', or any other kind of foolishness, I was right in on hit. I'd a-bet a man that red was green or that day was night, and if a gal had looked at me from a persimmon tree, why, law! I reckon I'd a-clumb the tree to git her. That's jest the way hit was with me all through the war. I never made a bet or played a game of cards in my life before the war or after hit was over, but while the war was goin' on I was ready fer anything.

"How much will you bet?" I said.

"I'll bet you a hundred dollars even money," said Bob Saunders, and no sooner got the words out of his mouth than the bet was on.

We planked the money down right thar and gave hit to Jim to hold the stakes. Well, sir, we didn't have to wait half an hour before a feller on a horse came ridin' up and told us hit was no use goin' any father—Fort Donelson had fallen.

"What did I tell you?" I said to Cap'n Saunders, and I put the money in my pocket.

Well, the laugh was on him then. I wish you could a-seen the expression on his face—he looked mighty sheepish, I tell you. But he admitted hit, you know, he had to own up.

"You were right," he said. "You won the bet. But—I'll tell you what I'll do!" He put his hand into his pocket and pulled out a roll of bills. "I've got a hundred dollars left—and with me hit's all or nothin'! We'll draw cards fer this last hundred, mine against yorn—high card wins!"

Well, I was ready fer him. I pulled out my hundred, and I said, "Git out the deck!"

So they brought the deck out then and Jim Weaver shuffled hit and held hit while we drew. Bob Saunders drawed first and he drawed the eight of spades. When I turned my card up I had one of the queens.

Well, sir, you should have seen the look upon Bob Saunders' face. I tell you what, the fellers whooped and hollered till he looked like he was ready to crawl through a hole in the floor. We all had some fun with him, and then, of course, I gave the money back. I never kept a penny in my life I made from gamblin'.

But that's the way hit was with me in those days—I was ready fer hit—fer anything. If any kind of devilment or foolishness came up I was right in on hit with the ringleaders.

Well then, Fort Donelson was the funniest fight that I was ever in because hit was all fun fer me without no fightin'. And that jest suited me. And Stone Mountain was the most peculiar fight that I was in because—well, I'll tell you a strange story and you can figger fer yourself if you ever heared about a fight like that before.

Did you ever hear of a battle in which one side never fired a shot and yet won the fight and did more damage and more destruction to the other side than all the guns and cannon in the world could do? Well, that was the battle of Stone Mountain. Now, I was in a lot of battles. But the battle of Stone Mountain was the queerest one of the whole war.

I'll tell you how hit was.

We was up on top of the Mountain and the Yankees was below us tryin' to drive us out and take the Mountain. We couldn't git our guns up thar, we didn't try to—we didn't have to git our guns up thar. The only gun I ever seed up thar was a little brass howitzer that we pulled up with ropes, but we never fired a shot with hit. We didn't git a chance to use hit. We no more'n got hit in position before a shell exploded right on top of hit and split that little howitzer plumb in two. Hit jest fell into two parts: you couldn't have made a neater job of hit if you'd cut hit down the middle with a saw. I'll never fergit that little howitzer and the way they split hit plumb in two.

As for the rest of the fightin' on our side, hit was done with rocks and stones. We gathered together a great pile of rocks and stones and boulders all along the top of the Mountain, and when they attacked we waited and let 'em have hit.

The Yankees attacked in three lines, one after the other. We waited until the first line was no more'n thirty feet below us—until we could see the whites of their eyes, as the sayin' goes—and then we let 'em have hit. We jest rolled those boulders down on 'em, and I tell you what, hit was an awful thing to watch. I never saw no worse destruction than that with guns and cannon during the whole war.

You could hear 'em screamin' and hollerin' until hit made your blood run cold. They kept comin' on and we mowed 'em down by the hundreds. We mowed 'em down without firin' a single shot. We crushed them, wiped them out—jest by rollin' those big rocks and boulders down on them.

There was bigger battles in the war, but Stone Mountain was the queerest one I ever seed.

Fort Donelson came early in the war, and Stone Mountain came later toward the end. And one was funny and the other was peculiar, but thar was fightin' in between that wasn't neither one. I'm goin' to tell you about that.

Fort Donelson was the first big fight that we was in—and as I say, we wasn't really in hit because we couldn't git to her in time. And after Donelson that spring, in April, thar was Shiloh. Well—all that I can tell you is, we was thar on time at Shiloh. Oh Lord, I reckon that we was! Perhaps we had been country boys before, perhaps some of us still made a joke of hit before—but after Shiloh we wasn't country boys no longer. We didn't make a joke about hit after Shiloh. They wiped the smile off of our faces at Shiloh. And after Shiloh we was boys no longer: we was vet'ran men.

From then on hit was fightin' to the end. That's where we learned what hit was like—at Shiloh. From then on we knowed what hit would be until the end.

Jim got wounded thar at Shiloh. Hit wasn't bad—not bad enough to suit him anyways—fer he wanted to go home fer good. Hit was a flesh wound in the leg, but hit was some time before they could git to him, and he was layin' out thar in the field and I reckon that he lost some blood. Anyways, he was unconscious when they picked him up. They carried him back and dressed his wound right thar upon the field. They cleaned hit out, I reckon, and they bandaged hit—thar was so many of 'em they couldn't do much more than that.

91

Oh, I tell you what, in those days thar wasn't much that they could do. I've seed the surgeons workin' underneath an open shed with meat-saws, choppin' off the arms and legs and throwin' 'em out thar in a pile like they was sticks of wood, sometimes without no chloroform or nothin', and the screamin' and the hollerin' of the men was enough to make your head turn gray. And that was as much as anyone could do. Hit was live or die and take your chance—and thar was so many of 'em wounded so much worse than Jim that I reckon he was lucky they did anything fer him at all.

I heared 'em tell about hit later, how he came to, a-lyin' stretched out thar on an old dirty blanket on the bare floor, and an army surgeon seed him lookin' at his leg all bandaged up and I reckon thought he'd cheer him up and said: "Oh, that ain't nothin'—you'll be up and fightin' Yanks again in two weeks' time."

Well, with that, they said, Jim got to cursin' and a-takin' on something terrible. They said the language he used was enough to make your hair stand up on end. They said he screamed and raved and reached down thar and jerked that bandage off and said—"Like hell I will!" They said the blood spouted up thar like a fountain, and they said that army doctor was so mad he throwed Jim down upon his back and sat on him and he took that bandage, all bloody as hit was, and he tied hit back around his leg again and he said: "Goddam you, if you pull that bandage off again, I'll let you bleed to death."

And Jim, they said, came ragin' back at him until you could have heared him fer a mile, and said: "Well, by God, I don't care if I do; I'd rather die than stay here any longer."

They say they had hit back and forth thar until Jim got so weak he couldn't talk no more. I know that when I come to see him a day or two later he was settin' up and I asked him: "Jim, how is your leg? Are you hurt bad?"

And he answered: "Not bad enough. They can take the whole damn leg off," he said, "as far as I'm concerned, and bury hit here at Shiloh if they'll only let me go back home and not come back again. Me and Martha will git along somehow," he said. "I'd rather be a cripple the rest of my life than have to come back and fight in this damn war."

Well, I knowed he meant hit too. I looked at him and seed how much he meant hit, and I knowed thar wasn't anything that I could do. When a man begins to talk that way, thar hain't much you can say to him. Well, sure enough, in a week or two, they let him go upon a two months' furlough and he went limpin' away upon a crutch. He was the happiest man I ever seed. "They gave me two months' leave," he said, "but if they jest let me git back home old Bragg'll have to send his whole damn army before he gits me out of thar again."

Well, he was gone two months or more, and I never knowed what happened—whether he got ashamed of himself when his wound healed up all right, or whether Martha talked him out of hit. But he was back with us again by late July—the grimmest, bitterest-lookin' man you ever seed. He wouldn't talk to me about hit, he wouldn't tell me what had happened, but I knowed from that time on he'd never draw his breath in peace until he left the army and got back home fer good.

Well, that was Shiloh, that was the time we didn't miss, that was where we lost our grin, where we knowed at last what hit would be until the end.

I've told you of three battles now, and one was funny, one was strange, and one was—well, one showed us what war and fightin' could be like. But I'll tell you of a fourth one now. And the fourth one was the greatest of the lot.

We seed some big fights in the war. And we was in some bloody battles. But the biggest fight we fought was Chickamauga. The bloodiest fight I ever seed was Chickamauga. Thar was big battles in the war, but thar never was a fight before, thar'll never be a fight again, like Chickamauga. I'm goin' to tell you how hit was at Chickamauga.

All through the spring and summer of that year Old Rosey follered us through Tennessee.

We had him stopped the year before, the time we whupped him at Stone's River at the end of '62. We tard him out so bad he had to wait. He waited thar six months at Murfreesboro. But we knowed he was a-comin' all the time. Old Rosey started at the end of June and drove us out to Shelbyville. We fell back on Tullahoma in rains the like of which you never seed. The rains that fell the last week in June that year was terrible. But Rosey kept a-comin' on.

He drove us out of Tullahoma too. We fell back across the Cumberland, we pulled back behind the mountain, but he follered us.

I reckon thar was fellers that was quicker when a fight was on, and when they'd seed just what hit was they had to do. But when it came to plannin' and a-figgerin', Old Rosey Rosecrans took the cake. Old Rosey was a fox. Fer sheer natural cunnin' I never knowed the beat of him.

While Bragg was watchin' him at Chattanooga to keep him from gittin' across the Tennessee, he sent some fellers forty mile up stream. And then he'd march 'em back and forth and round the hill and back in front of us again where we could look at 'em, until you'd a-thought that every Yankee in the world was there. But laws! All that was just a dodge! He had fellers a-sawin't and a-hammerin', a-buildin' boats, a-blowin' bugles and a-beatin' drums, makin' all the noise they could—you could hear 'em over yonder gittin' ready—and all the time Old Rosey was fifty mile or more down stream, ten mile past Chattanooga, a-fixin' to git over way down thar. That was the kind of feller Rosey was.

We reached Chattanooga early in July and waited fer two months. Old Rosey hadn't caught up with us yet. He still had to cross the Cumberland, push his men and pull his trains across the ridges and through the gaps before he got to us. July went by, we had no news of him. "Oh Lord!" said Jim, "perhaps he ain't a-comin'!" I knowed he was a-comin', but I let Jim have his way.

Some of the fellers would git used to hit. A feller'd git into a frame of mind where he wouldn't let hit worry him. He'd let termorrer look out fer hitself. That was the way hit was with me.

With Jim hit was the other way around. Now that he knowed Martha Patton he was a different man. I think he hated the war and army life from the moment that he met her. From that time he was livin' only fer one thing—to go back home and marry that gal. When mail would come and some of us was gittin' letters he'd be the first in line; and if she wrote him why he'd walk away like someone in a dream. And if she failed to write he'd jest go off somers and set down by himself: he'd be in such a state of misery he didn't want to talk to no one. He got the reputation with the fellers fer bein' queer—unsociable—always a-broodin' and a-frettin' about somethin' and a-wantin' to be left alone. And so, after a time, they let him be. He wasn't popular with most of them—but they never knowed what was wrong, they never knowed that he wasn't really the way they thought he was at all. Hit was jest that he was hit so desperate hard, the worst-in-love man that I ever seed. But law! I knowed what was the trouble from the start.

Hit's funny how war took a feller. Before the war I was the serious one, and Jim had been the one to play.

I reckon that I'd had to work too hard. We was so poor. Before the war hit almost seemed I never knowed the time I didn't have to work. And when the war came, why I only thought of all the fun and frolic I was goin' to have; and then at last, when I knowed what hit was like, why I was used to hit and didn't care.

I always could git used to things. And I reckon maybe that's the reason that I'm here. I wasn't one to worry much, and no matter how rough the goin' got I always figgered I could hold out if the others could. I let termorrer look out fer hitself. I reckon that you'd have to say I was an optimist. If things got bad, well, I always figgered that they could be worse; and if they got so bad they couldn't be no worse, why then I'd figger that they couldn't last this way ferever, they'd have to git some better sometime later on.

I reckon toward the end thar, when they got so bad we didn't think they'd ever git no better, I'd reached the place where I jest didn't care. I could still lay down and go to sleep and not worry over what was goin' to come termorrer, because I never knowed what was to come and so I didn't let hit worry me. I reckon you'd have to say that was the Pentland in me—our belief in what we call predestination.

Now, Jim was jest the other way. Before the war he was happy as a lark and thought of nothin' except havin' fun. But then the war came and hit changed him so you wouldn't a-knowed he was the same man.

And, as I say, hit didn't happen all at once. Jim was the happiest man I ever seed that mornin' that we started out from home. I reckon he thought of the war as we all did, as a big frolic. We gave hit jest about six months. We figgered we'd be back by then, and of course all that jest suited Jim. I reckon that suited all of us. It would give us all a chance to wear a uniform and to see the world, to shoot some Yankees and to run 'em north, and then to come back home and lord it over those who hadn't been and be a hero and court the gals.

That was the way hit looked to us when we set out from Zebulon. We never thought about the winter. We never thought about the mud and cold and rain. We never knowed what hit would be to have to march on an empty belly, to have to march barefoot with frozen feet and with no coat upon your back, to have to lay down on bare ground and try to sleep with no coverin' above you, and thankful half the time if you could find dry ground to sleep upon, and too tard the rest of hit to care. We never knowed or thought about such things as these. We never knowed how hit would be there in the cedar thickets beside Chickamauga Creek. And if we had a-knowed, if someone had a-told us, why I reckon that none of us would a-cared. We was too young and ignorant to care. And as fer knowin't—law! The only trouble about knowin' is that you've got to know what knowin's like before you know what knowin' is. Thar's no one that can tell you. You've got to know hit fer yourself.

Well, like I say, we'd been fightin' all this time and still thar was no sign of the war endin'. Old Rosey jest kept a-follerin' us and—"Lord!" Jim would say, "will it never end?"

I never knowed myself. We'd been fightin' fer two years, and I'd given over knowin' long ago. With Jim hit was different. He'd been a-praying and a-hopin' from the first that soon hit would be over and that he could go back and get that gal. And at first, fer a year or more, I tried to cheer him up. I told him that it couldn't last forever. But after a while hit wasn't no use to tell him that. He wouldn't believe me any longer.

Because Old Rosey kept a-comin' on. We'd whup him and we'd stop him fer a while, but then he'd git his wind, he'd be on our trail again, he'd drive us back.—"Oh Lord!" said Jim, "will hit never stop?"

That summer I been tellin' you about, he drove us down through Tennessee. He drove us out of Shelbyville, and we fell back on Tullahoma, to the passes of the hills. When we pulled back across the Cumberland I said to Jim: "Now we've got him. He'll have to cross the mountains now to git at us. And when he does, we'll have him. That's all that Bragg's been waitin' fer. We'll whup the daylights out of him this time," I said, "and after that thar'll be nothin' left of him. We'll be home by Christmas, Jim—you wait and see."

And Jim just looked at me and shook his head and said: "Lord, Lord, I don't believe this war'll ever end!"

Hit wasn't that he was afraid—or, if he was, hit made a wildcat of him in the fightin'. Jim could get fightin' mad like no one else I ever seed. He could do things, take chances no one else I ever knowed would take. But I reckon hit was jest because he was so desperate. He hated hit so much. He couldn't git used to hit the way the others could. He couldn't take hit as hit came. Hit wasn't so much that he was afraid to die. I guess hit was that he was still so full of livin'. He didn't want to die because he wanted to live so much. And he wanted to live so much because he was in love.

...So, like I say, Old Rosey finally pushed us back across the Cumberland. He was in Chattanooga in July, and fer a few weeks hit was quiet thar. But all the time I knowed that Rosey would keep comin' on. We got wind of him again along in August. He had started after us again. He pushed his trains across the Cumberland, with the roads so bad, what with the rains, his wagons sunk down to the axle hubs. But he got 'em over, came down in the valley, then across the ridge, and early in September he was on our heels again.

We cleared out of Chattanooga on the eighth. And our tail end was pullin' out at one end of the town as Rosey came in through the other. We dropped down around the mountain south of town and Rosey thought he had us on the run again.

But this time he was fooled. We was ready fer him now, a-pickin' out our spot and layin' low. Old Rosey follered us. He sent McCook around down toward the south to head us off. He thought he had us in retreat but when McCook got thar we wasn't thar at all. We'd come down south of town and taken our positions along Chickamauga Creek. McCook had gone too far. Thomas was follerin' us from the north and when McCook tried to git back to join Thomas, he couldn't pass us, fer we blocked the way. They had to fight us or be cut in two.

We was in position on the Chickamauga on the seventeenth. The Yankees streamed in on the eighteenth, and took their position in the woods a-facin' us. We had our backs to Lookout Mountain and the Chickamauga Creek. The Yankees had their line thar in the woods before us on a rise, with Missionary Ridge behind them to the east.

The Battle of Chickamauga was fought in a cedar thicket. That cedar thicket, from what I knowed of hit, was about three miles long and one mile wide. We fought fer two days all up and down that thicket and to and fro across hit. When the fight started that cedar thicket was so thick and dense you could a-took a butcher knife and drove hit in thar anywhere and hit would a-stuck. And when that fight was over that cedar thicket had been so destroyed by shot and shell you could a-looked in thar anywheres with your naked eye and seed a black snake run a hundred yards away. If you'd a-looked at that cedar thicket the day after that fight was over you'd a-wondered how a hummin' bird the size of your thumbnail could a-flown through thar without bein' torn into pieces by the fire. And yet more than half of us who went into that thicket came out of hit alive and tole the tale. You wouldn't have thought that hit was possible. But I was thar and seed hit, and hit was.

A little after midnight—hit may have been about two o'clock that mornin', while we lay there waitin' for the fight we knowed was bound to come next day—Jim woke me up. I woke up like a flash—you got used to hit in those days—and though hit was so dark you could hardly see your hand a foot away, I knowed his face at once. He was white as a ghost and he had got thin as a rail in that last year's campaign. In the dark his face looked white as paper. He dug his hand into my arm so hard hit hurt. I roused up sharp-like; then I seed him and knowed who hit was.

"John!" he said—"John!"—and he dug his fingers in my arm so hard he made hit ache—"John! I've seed him! He was here again!"

I tell you what, the way he said hit made my blood run cold. They say we Pentlands are a superstitious people, and perhaps we are. They told hit how they saw my brother George a-comin' up the hill one day at sunset, how they all went out upon the porch and waited fer him, how everyone, the children and the grown-ups alike, all seed him as he clumb the hill, and how he passed behind a tree and disappeared as if the ground had swallered him—and how they got the news ten days later that he'd been killed at Chancellorsville on that very day and hour. I've heared these stories and I know the others all believe them, but I never put no stock in them myself. And yet, I tell you what! The sight of that white face and those black eyes a-burnin' at me in the dark—the way he said hit and the way hit was—fer I could feel the men around me and hear somethin' movin' in the wood—I heared a trace chain rattle and hit was enough to make your blood run cold! I grabbed hold of him—I shook him by the arm—I didn't want the rest of 'em to hear—I told him to hush up—

"John, he was here!" he said.

I never asked him what he meant—I knowed too well to ask. It was the third time he'd seed hit in a month—a man upon a horse. I didn't want to hear no more—I told him that hit was a dream and I told him to go back to sleep.

"I tell you, John, hit was no dream!" he said. "Oh John I heared hit—and I heared his horse—and I seed him sittin' thar as plain as day—and he never said a word to me—he jest sat thar lookin' down, and then he turned and rode away into the woods....John, John, I heared him and I don't know what hit means!"

Well, whether he seed hit or imagined hit or dreamed hit, I don't know. But the sight of his black eyes a-burnin' holes through me in the dark made me feel almost as if I'd seed hit, too. I told him to lay down by me—and still I seed his eyes a-blazin' thar. I know he didn't sleep a wink the rest of that whole night. I closed my eyes and tried to make him think that I was sleepin' but hit was no use—we lay thar wide awake. And both of us was glad when mornin' came.

The fight began upon our right at ten o'clock. We couldn't find out what was happenin': the woods thar was so close and thick we never knowed fer two days what had happened, and we didn't know fer certain then. We never knowed how many we was fightin' or how many we had lost. I've heared them say that even Old Rosey himself didn't know jest what had happened when he rode back into town next day, and didn't know that Thomas was still standin' like a rock. And if Old Rosey didn't know no more than this about hit, what could a common soldier know? We fought back and forth across that cedar thicket for two days, and thar was times when you would be right up on top of them before you even knowed that they was thar. And that's the way the fightin' went—the bloodiest fightin' that was ever knowed, until that cedar thicket was soaked red with blood, and thar was hardly a place left in thar where a sparrer could have perched.

And as I say, we heared 'em fightin' out upon our right at ten o'clock, and then the fightin' came our way. I heared later that this fightin' started when the Yanks come down to the Creek and run into a bunch of Forrest's men and drove 'em back. And then they had hit back and forth until they got drove back themselves, and that's the way we had hit all day long. We'd attack and we'd beat them off. And that was the way hit went from mornin' till night. We piled up there upon their left: they mowed us down with canister and grape until the very grass was soakin' with our blood, but we kept comin' on. We must have charged a dozen times that day—I was in four of 'em myself. We fought back and forth across that wood until there wasn't a piece of hit as big as the palm of your hand we hadn't fought on. We busted through their right at two-thirty in the afternoon and got way over past the Widder Glenn's, where Rosey had his quarters, and beat 'em back until we got the whole way 'cross the Lafayette Road and took possession of the road. And then they drove us out again. And we kept comin' on, and both sides were still at hit after darkness fell.

We fought back and forth across that road all day with first one side and then the t'other holdin' hit until that road itself was soaked in blood. They called that road the Bloody Lane, and that was jest the name fer it.

We kept fightin' an hour or more after hit had gotten dark, and you could see the rifles flashin' in the woods, but then hit all died down. I tell you what, that night was somethin' to remember and to marvel at as long as you live. The fight had set the wood afire in places, and you could see the smoke and flames and hear the screamin' and the hollerin' of the wounded until hit made your blood run cold. We got as many as we could—but some we didn't even try to git—we jest let 'em lay. It was an awful thing to hear. I reckon many a wounded man was jest left to die or burn to death because we couldn't git 'em out.

You could see the nurses and the stretcher-bearers movin' through the woods, and each side huntin' fer hits dead. You could see them movin' in the smoke an' flames, an' you could see the dead men layin' there as thick as wheat, with their corpse-like faces 'n black powder on their lips, an' a little bit of moonlight comin' through the trees, and all of hit more like a nightmare out of hell than anything I ever knowed before.

But we had other work to do. All through the night we could hear the Yanks a-choppin' and a-thrashin' round, and we knowed that they was fellin' trees to block us when we went fer them next mornin'. Fer we knowed the fight was only jest begun. We figgered that we'd had the best of hit, but we knowed no one had won the battle yet. We knowed the second day would beat the first.

Jim knowed hit too. Poor Jim, he didn't sleep that night—he never seed the man upon the horse that night he jest sat there, a-grippin' his knees and starin', and a-sayin', "Lord God, Lord God, when will hit ever end?"

Then mornin' came at last. This time we knowed jest where we was and what hit was we had to do. Our line was fixed by that time. Bragg knowed at last where Rosey had his line, and Rosey knowed where we was. So we waited there, both sides, till mornin' came. Hit was a foggy mornin' with mist upon the ground. Around ten o'clock when the mist began to rise, we got the order and we went chargin' through the wood again.

We knowed the fight was goin' to be upon the right— upon our right, that is—on Rosey's left. And we knowed that Thomas was in charge on Rosey's left. And we all knowed that hit was easier to crack a flint rock with your teeth than to make old Thomas budge. But we went after him, and I tell you what, that was a fight! The first day's fight had been like playin' marbles when compared to this.

We hit old Thomas on his left at half-past ten, and Breckenridge came sweepin' round and turned old Thomas's flank and came in at his back, and then we had hit hot and heavy. Old Thomas whupped his men around like he would crack a raw-hide whup and drove Breckenridge back around the flank again, but we was back on top of him before you knowed the first attack was over.

The fight went ragin' down the flank, down to the center of Old Rosey's army and back and forth across the left, and all up and down old Thomas's line. We'd hit him right and left and in the middle, and he'd come back at us and throw us back again. And we went ragin' back and forth thar like two bloody lions with that cedar thicket so tore up, so bloody and so thick with dead by that time, that hit looked as if all hell had broken loose in thar.

Rosey kept a-whuppin' men around off of his right, to help old Thomas on the left to stave us off. And then we'd hit old Thomas left of center and we'd bank him in the middle and we'd hit him on his left again, and he'd whup those Yankees back and forth off of the right into his flanks and middle as we went fer him, until we run those Yankees ragged. We had them gallopin' back and forth like kangaroos, and in the end that was the thing that cooked their goose.

The worst fightin' had been on the left, on Thomas's line, but to hold us thar they'd thinned their right out and had failed to close in on the center of their line. And at two o'clock that afternoon when Longstreet seed the gap in Wood's position on the right, he took five brigades of us and poured us through. That whupped them. That broke their line and smashed their whole right all to smithereens. We went after them like a pack of ragin' devils. We killed 'em and we took 'em by the thousands, and those we didn't kill and take right thar went streamin' back across the Ridge as if all hell was at their heels.

That was a rout if ever I heared tell of one! They went streamin' back across the Ridge—hit was each man fer himself and the devil take the hindmost. They caught Rosey comin' up—he rode into them—he tried to check 'em, face 'em round, and get 'em to come on again—hit was like tryin' to swim the Mississippi upstream on a boneyard mule! They swept him back with them as if he'd been a wooden chip. They went streamin' into Rossville like the rag-tag of creation—the worst whupped army that you ever seed, and Old Rosey was along with all the rest!

He knowed hit was all up with him, or thought he knowed hit, for everybody told him the Army of the Cumberland had been blowed to smithereens and that hit was a general rout. And Old Rosey turned and rode to Chattanooga, and he was a beaten man. I've heared tell that when he rode up to his headquarters thar in Chattanooga they had to help him from his horse, and that he walked into the house all dazed and fuddled-like, like he never knowed what had happened to him—and that he jest sat thar struck dumb and never spoke.

This was at four o'clock of that same afternoon. And then the news was brought to him that Thomas was still thar upon the field and wouldn't budge. Old Thomas stayed thar like a rock. We'd smashed the right, we'd sent it flyin' back across the Ridge, the whole Yankee right was broken into bits and streamin' back to Rossville for dear life. Then we bent old Thomas back upon his left. We thought we had him, he'd have to leave the field or else surrender. But old Thomas turned and fell back along the Ridge and put his back against the wall thar, and he wouldn't budge.

Longstreet pulled us back at three o'clock when we had broken up the right and sent them streamin' back across the Ridge. We thought that hit was over then. We moved back stumblin' like men walkin' in a dream. And I turned to Jim—I put my arm around him, and I said: "Jim, what did I say? I knowed hit, we've licked 'em and this is the end!" I never even knowed if he heard me. He went stumblin' on beside me with his face as white as paper and his lips black with the powder of the cartridge-bite, mumblin' and mutterin' to himself like someone talkin' in a dream. And we fell back to position, and they told us all to rest. And we leaned thar on our rifles like men who hardly knowed if they had come out of that hell alive or dead.

"Oh Jim, we've got 'em and this is the end!" I said.

He leaned thar swayin' on his rifle, starin' through the wood. He jest leaned and swayed thar, and he never said a word, and those great eyes of his a-burnin' through the wood.

"Jim, don't you hear me?"—and I shook him by the arm. "Hit's over, man! We've licked 'em and the fight is over!—Can't you understand?"

And then I heared them shoutin' on the right, the word came down the line again, and Jim—poor Jim!—he raised his head and listened, and "Oh God!" he said, "we've got to go again!"

Well, hit was true. The word had come that Thomas had lined up on the Ridge, and we had to go fer him again. After that I never exactly knowed what happened. Hit was like fightin' in a bloody dream—like doin' somethin' in a nightmare—only the nightmare was like death and hell. Longstreet threw us up that hill five times, I think, before darkness came. We'd charge up to the very muzzles of their guns, and they'd mow us down like grass, and we'd come stumblin' back—or what was left of us—and form again at the foot of the hill, and then come on again. We'd charge right up the Ridge and drive 'em through the gap and fight 'em with cold steel, and they'd come back again and we'd brain each other with the butt end of our guns. Then they'd throw us back and we'd re-form and come on after 'em again.

The last charge happened jest at dark. We came along and stripped the ammunition off the dead—we took hit from the wounded—we had nothin' left ourselves. Then we hit the first line—and we drove them back. We hit the second and swept over them. We were goin' up to take the third and last—they waited till they saw the color of our eyes before they let us have hit. Hit was like a river of red-hot lead had poured down on us: the line melted thar like snow. Jim stumbled and spun round as if somethin' had whupped him like a top. He fell right toward me, with his eyes wide open and the blood a-pourin' from his mouth. I took one look at him and then stepped over him like he was a log. Thar was no more to see or think of now—no more to reach—except that line. We reached hit and they let us have hit—and we stumbled back.

And yet we knowed that we had won a victory. That's what they told us later—and we knowed hit must be so because when daybreak came next mornin' the Yankees was all gone. They had all retreated into town, and we was left there by the Creek at Chickamauga in possession of the field.

I don't know how many men got killed. I don't know which side lost the most. I only know you could have walked across the dead men without settin' foot upon the ground. I only know that cedar thicket which had been so dense and thick two days before you could've drove a knife into hit and hit would of stuck, had been so shot to pieces that you could've looked in thar on Monday mornin' with your naked eye and seed a black snake run a hundred yards away.

I don't know how many men we lost or how many of the Yankees we may have killed. The Generals on both sides can figger all that out to suit themselves. But I know that when that fight was over you could have looked in thar and wondered how a hummin' bird could've flown through that cedar thicket and come out alive. And yet that happened, yes, and something more than hummin' birds—fer men came out, alive.

And on that Monday mornin', when I went back up the Ridge to where Jim lay, thar just beside him on a little torn piece of bough, I heard a redbird sing. I turned Jim over and got his watch, his pocket-knife, and what few papers and belongin's that he had, and some letters that he'd had from Martha Patton. And I put them in my pocket.

And then I got up and looked around. It all seemed funny after hit had happened, like something that had happened in a dream. Fer Jim had wanted so desperate hard to live, and hit had never mattered half so much to me, and now I was a-standin' thar with Jim's watch and Martha Patton's letters in my pocket and a-listenin' to that little redbird sing.

And I would go all through the war and go back home and marry Martha later on, and fellers like poor Jim was layin' thar at Chickamauga Creek.

Hit's all so strange now when you think of hit. Hit all turned out so different from the way we thought. And that was long ago, and I'll be ninety-five years old if I am livin' on the seventh day of August of this present year. Now that's goin' back a long ways, hain't hit? And yet hit all comes back to me as clear as if hit happened yesterday. And then hit all will go away and be as strange as if hit happened in a dream.

But I have been in some big battles I can tell you. I've seen strange things and been in bloody fights. But the biggest fight that I was ever in—the bloodiest battle anyone has ever fought—was at Chickamauga in that cedar thicket—at Chickamauga Creek in that great war.

The Rebel Trace

Joseph Hergesheimer

At dusk, in the barren mountains of Eastern Kentucky, an aide galloped up to the head of the third brigade of General Morgan's Confederate force. Wickliffe Sash, captain in the first battalion, was walking beside Colonel Smith, in immediate command.

"We will rest here for the night," the aide said, with a shadowy salute. "General Morgan's order."

That decision, Wickliffe told himself, had not come too soon by a moment. His company was practically incapable of another step. He returned to it.

"Fall out," he ordered.

The men collapsed where they were. Behind them the precarious way—the Rebel Trace—vanished in an abrupt turn around a high bare shoulder of mountain; they had come upon a contracted open space where, clinging to steep walls of stone, there were some scattered melancholy pine trees and a swift narrow stream; ahead, Wickliffe could see nothing but a rocky defile rapidly growing dark. The stream made a loud impetuous sound and a whippoorwill called and called from a pine tree.

The first two brigades were mounted, but the third brigade was on foot—it had been composed of the men for whom no mounts could be provided. Wickliffe, however, was unable to decide if that were a disadvantage or a benefit.

The animals had suffered more than the men—Colonel Giltner's brigade alone had lost at least two hundred horses. Morgan's mounted infantry, it seemed to him, had become foot cavalry. At any rate, the third battalion had kept up with the men on horseback.

He said to Major Diamond, "I don't like the way the men look. They are not taking care of themselves. Their feet are cut to pieces."

What, Major Diamond inquired, could they expect? "A hundred and fifty miles of these mountains in seven days. Worse than twenty miles a day climbing in formation. Some only left Huyter's Gap ten days ago. That's two hundred miles anyhow."

Wickliffe saw that Diamond was discouraged. His own feet were so swollen that he didn't think his boots would come off.

He moved back to where his company lay in a variety of exhausted attitudes on the mountainside.

"Where is the kitchen detail?" he demanded. "Ambrose Huffman!" he called. "Where is Ambrose?" A short figure, fat and inexpressibly weary-looking, rose. "Get supper started," Wickliffe ordered him. "Send two men for wood and two for water. We want coffee before morning."

It was little use, Huffman replied, to prepare supper. "There won't be nobody hardly to want it. Captain Sash, it's God's truth; the boys are too tired to eat. Most of them are asleep right now."

"I want two men to go for wood and two with buckets for water," Wickliffe Sash repeated harshly. "You have forty-five minutes to make a mess of bread and boil bacon and greens, if we have any. With coffee. Lieutenant Brenno." First Lieutenant Jacob Brenno stood at an uncertain attention. "Send up the usual picket detail to the brigade head. The rest can stay where they are for half an hour. Then get them in line for supper. Everyone, Mr. Brenno. If Ambrose Huffman isn't ready, from now on he'll do with a musket instead of a frying pan. In the front rank. It won't matter to me if we lose a good cook."

Wickliffe sat on a small ledge of rock. He was, like Major Diamond, filled with doubts.

What day was it? It was the seventh day of June in 1864. They had reached Pound Gap, beyond the Virginia line, on the second, after dislodging the small Union force guarding that entrance to Kentucky. General Morgan absolutely counted on investing Mount Sterling tomorrow. He had no time to lose. When it was discovered that he was again raiding in Kentucky—it must be known to the Union headquarters in the state tomorrow—there would be an overwhelming concentration of troops upon him. General Hobson, with six regiments of cavalry, three thousand strong, was with Burbridge and part of the Twenty-third Union Army Corps somewhere near Louisa, south of Pound Gap. General Averell and General Crook were on the march. General Burbridge would not linger in the east. Morgan, at best, had twenty-five hundred men. His success depended upon the outcome of the race between the Federal commander and himself for Mount Sterling. The distance was greater for General Burbridge, and he was hampered with artillery; Morgan had no cannon, but his brigades were weary from the immediate exhausting past.

The odds against him, Wickliffe knew, were not important. This was Morgan's fourth raid into Kentucky—a state that had remained part of the North—and he had always been opposed to enormous majorities of men and arms. On the whole, successfully. John Hunt Morgan was a military genius. Everyone, North and South, acknowledged that. It belonged to his genius to make his force seem larger, infinitely more threatening, than it ever actually was. He split his command into small detachments and sent them here and there against towns and stockades and railway bridges and bases of Federal supplies. These individual assaults were made with great swiftness and the bodies of men composing them swiftly returned to the main body of troops. It was a further characteristic of General Morgan that all his engagements were fought upon the advance. When he retreated he retreated. Morgan didn't, then, stop for anything. That was why he still, after three years, had a command at all; why they were not all either killed or in Northern prisons.

The best of so much, Wickliffe Sash realized, belonged in the past. To the first and second raids, and even to the disastrous third raid into Indiana and Ohio, when John Morgan had been captured. Yes, it was different now, with the unavoidable multiplication of his reverses. It was different, worse, with the whole Confederacy. Wickliffe, sitting on cold rock in the fast-gathering darkness, his body one intolerable ache, said to himself, "We are licked." He said it and, deep within him, he knew it was true, but he would not acknowledge it. "A miracle will save us," Wickliffe Sash added. "England will recognize the Confederacy, the blockade will fail; a miracle—General Lee—will save us." But Morgan's situation was desperate. This must be his final raid and it must succeed. He was, for one thing, losing his prestige with the soldiers on paper. With President Davis and Richmond. They would not admit, through ignorance and jealousy, the enormous good General Morgan had worked in Kentucky. Again and again he had diverted, more than once actually scattered, the concentration of armies bent on the destruction of the Confederate resources and commands in Tennessee and in Southern Virginia.

If Morgan failed now, it would be over with him. All Wickliffe Sash's weariness, his doubts, were lost sight of in his passionate realization that they must reach Mount Sterling before General Burbridge could get there. Before the Union forces had time to close around them.

On his left the kitchen fires made a sullen glow on the accomplished night. He could see the fires of companies ahead of him. There was an occasional call and the distant scrape of horses' hoofs, a scarce-moving figure—the brigades were largely silent and he could hear no singing. The strains of Stump-tailed Dolly and of General Stuart's favorite song, If You Want to Have Fun, Jine the Cavalry, were wholly absent. He could, now, hear Lieutenant Brenno stirring among the men of their company.

"Line up for mess!" Brenno cried. "Everyone on his feet!" There was a slow responding movement and a half-audible bitter cursing. Wickliffe Sash had a battered tin cup of coffee, a thin segment of bread hardly better than a burned paste of dough, and bacon boiled without greens.

Lieutenant Colonel Martin requested his presence, and Wickliffe found him with Alston, who commanded the second brigade, Colonel Giltner and General Morgan. Morgan, still a handsome figure, had his tunic unbuttoned and showed unmistakable traces of the continued strain on him. He had never, Wickliffe Sash believed, wholly recovered from his imprisonment on Johnson's Island. His voice was sharp and his periods short. The command was to move at daybreak. Its purposes, as usual, were diverse: Captain Jergens, with fifty men, would be detached to destroy the Frankfort and Louisville Railroad bridges. Major Chenowyeth would burn the railway bridges of the Kentucky Central. Captain Sash, who was especially familiar with the ground about Lexington, General Morgan required to proceed ahead with messages of his intentions to Confederate supporters in Fayette County.

In the morning there was a space of gray depression, the physical agony of all further movement, and then the sun enveloped Wickliffe Sash in a blaze of transcendent beauty. The mountains fell away behind him, their gloomy ascents and stone precipices dissolved, and before him lay a wide and brilliant and pastoral plain. There were, everywhere, noble groves and woodland meadows deep in grass, shaded by aged sugar trees and elms and hickory and tulip poplars; he saw orderly pastures with whitewashed fences where horses burnished by the sun were slowly grazing, with flowing tails and manes, red Devon cattle like animals in dark copper. The pastures were woven with crystal streams; houses, tranquil and white, were set in the tall groves, with lawns falling away in slopes and terraces of flowers; and everywhere the grass was bluer than green.

An intolerable sharp pain of recognition and longing, of relief, struck into Wickliffe. "The bluegrass," he said out loud. The peace and loveliness of the land below him, the great houses among the trees and the small houses along the roads, with the morning smoke rising from their chimneys, wet his face with sudden irrepressible tears. It was the bluegrass! It was home. The privations and terrors of war, the brazen noise and hailing iron and lead, the swift silent peril, seemed to have been lost with the mountains. No one, on that vast sweet plain of happiness and plenty, must need food or shelter or security. Wickliffe, as General Morgan had acknowledged, knew it intimately; he had caught innumerable silvery fish in its innumerable clear silver rivers; he had shot quail and woodcock in its thickets, squirrels and wild turkey in the woods and clearings; there was hardly a house of consequence where—when, before the war, he was a boy—he had not danced to the fiddling of negroes and added to the gayety of the barbecues.

A general revival of spirits possessed Morgan's column. The men shouted happily and called to one another their comments and appreciation of what, they would die to maintain, was the finest country God had ever made. There was a momentary relaxation of discipline, and then the files were closed, Morgan's marching formation was resumed. The advance guard rode four hundred yards ahead of the main body; posted at equal spaces of a hundred yards between it and the column were three vedettes; six vedettes were thrown out ahead of the guard, four at intervals of fifty yards and two, at a like distance, at the extreme front. Wickliffe Sash, mounted on the best horse the command could afford him—a pure-blooded bright bay—trotted past the battalions, the advance guard and the vedettes. He bore no signs of his rank or service; a heavy revolver, however, was plainly in sight at his belt; and he had caught up the wide brim of his dusty hat with a black plume. Wickliffe was, for local and immediate purposes, a member of the Union Home Guard. To what company he belonged depended upon who might stop him and where he was examined.

That character, his characterization, was not new to him; he had assumed it before—on General Morgan's December raid—in the region he knew best. The papers he carried—two minute communications—were hidden in two of the cartridges that supplied his revolver. Wickliffe Sash paid small attention to them or to the potentiality of his situation. It was a phase of war, and war had grown to be a commonplace of existence; he accepted its diverse responsibilities and dangers largely mechanically. He had, providentially, escaped any physical hurt; but so many of the men who had enlisted with him in the fall of 1861 had been killed, he had become so familiar with death and shocking injury, that he gave that finality only a perfunctory attention. There were moments still when fear touched him, but he regarded it as a distasteful finality in itself, and cast it off.

He left behind, at last, even the sound of Morgan's advance. Alone on the road that led toward Mount Sterling, Wickliffe's thoughts attached themselves solely to his cousin, Charlotte Hazel. In a very short while now he would be with her again for a few hours. Would this, he speculated, be a good time for their marriage? Mason Hazel, who had been forced by the death of his father to remain at Greenland, would be able to secure a preacher, sympathetic to the South, for the ceremony. Perhaps Charlotte, after all, must decide that. He would agree—he would always agree, Wickliffe added—with her wishes. She was a heavenly female creature. He remembered in every detail the evening when he had first addressed to her his love. It had occurred at a family party given by Mrs. Abel in Frankfort just when, for him, the war began. Charlotte at that time was thirteen years old. They had walked down through a rose arbor to the river bank, and there he had kissed her. There—a girlish kiss—she had kissed him. Wickliffe recalled the solemn tones of her voice: "I love you, Wickliffe, and nobody else, and I will marry only you." Within an hour he had gone to Lexington in an effort to prevent a shipment of arms from reaching Camp Robinson.

He had not seen Charlotte since then. He had been in Lexington, at Greenland, on the December raid, but she had been in Louisville. That, however, with her promise, was comparatively unimportant. "When I come home," he told himself, "now or later, Charlotte will marry me." Wickliffe Sash gazed down, entertained by the great fair beard spread across his chest. What would Charlotte think of it? She would, it was more than likely, insist that it must be cut off. Well, he couldn't do that at present; it was, in places unaccustomed to his new maturity, decidedly useful.

Wickliffe was, unobserved, riding hard; he came up to Mount Sterling and avoided the town by means of a side road upon the south. He planned to enter Lexington at dark.

Later his horse was finally exhausted, and he boldly demanded another at the stables of the Home Guard in Winchester. He was, he said, carrying dispatches from Mount Sterling to the Union leaders in Lexington—Morgan was raiding again. He had left his department in Virginia with more than nine thousand cavalry and was expected to reach Pound Gap in three days or better. Soon he was urging an ungainly but vigorous black animal steadily westward. No one stopped him; he proceeded without accident or observation. As he drew nearer to Lexington he became increasingly impatient to see Charlotte and once more kiss her. It seemed incredible that she should exist, so delicate and fragrant, in a world loud and barren and torn by war.

Lost in conjectures, in memory and anticipation, he came suddenly upon Lexington. It had a closed, almost deserted appearance; the lights in the Phoenix Hotel were dim and few; he proceeded deliberately over Broadway to Virgil Hunt's house. There, knocking the tops from the cartridges that held them, he delivered General Morgan's messages. It was very quiet in the bluegrass, he learned. Virgil Hunt considered that the moment, with General Hobson withdrawn from Mount Sterling and Burbridge absent, was favorable for Morgan's purpose.

"Life is suspended here," Virgil explained; "the streets in Lexington have the air of a funeral. The Yankee troops come and go; it has been two years almost since you were here. A Union regiment of cavalry, the Forty-fifth Kentucky, made Lexington their rendezvous in May. It was very social. Now, I believe, they are on the eastern front. I have seen something of your family—Calydon is closed; your mother is still in Montgomery; and I hear your father is at Richmond, attached to President Davis' staff. He never recovered from his saber wound at Missionary Ridge. It's hard to realize that both your brothers are gone, Wickliffe. Splendid boys if they did support the North. Your cousin, Elisha Abel, has been reported missing. I see Mrs. Abel on the streets in Lexington occasionally. A cold, self-contained woman. After Mansah Abel died, she never let Elisha out of her sight. But the war cured that." Wickliffe Sash rose. When did he plan to leave, Virgil Hunt asked.

"At once," Wickliffe told him; "I'll stop at Greenland and then go back to the column. It ought to be near. There wasn't much of a force at Mount Sterling. Well, we haven't much more. The details General Morgan sends out look like our main body."

Wickliffe Sash went beyond the main entrance to Greenland and followed a wood road, used by the farm wagons, that led from the Paris turnpike to the slave quarters and tobacco barn. He hitched his horse lightly to a rack there and walked over the rough sod, through the darkness, to the house. He was suddenly excited. A kitchen wing extended one wall of the Hazel dwelling backward: in the past it would have been brightly lighted, filled with a gay, self-important stir of negroes; now it was dark and silent. Wickliffe stood listening on the portico. The house was silent, the high doors, open upon the hall, showed a glimmer of light, probably a solitary whale-oil lamp, in the drawing-room at the left. He quietly entered the house. Mason Hazel was reading, Charlotte and their mother were sitting on a stiff black sofa.

Charlotte saw him first. She rose with a low exclamation, half frightened. Mason dropped his book and quickly secured a revolver from a table drawer. "Why," he said, relieved, "it's Wickliffe."

Wickliffe Sash hesitated before Charlotte; he could not make up his mind whether he ought to kiss her at once or wait until they were alone. An intangible impulse made him delay. In reality, he spoke properly to Mrs. Hazel first.

"I am glad to be back again," he said simply, taking one of her hands in both of his.

She was a small, rigidly held woman with fine white hair in a cap of fine lace, and a high-bridged autocratic nose. Mrs. Hazel belonged to a celebrated Kentucky family; she was wholly devoted to the cause of the South; these were facts that she permitted no one to diminish; and Wickliffe saw that, in the face of the repeated disasters both to her family and the Confederacy, she was, if anything, stiffer in pride and certainty than ever.

He was, at the same time, vaguely conscious of a strangeness of manner in her. If it were possible for Mrs. Archelaus Hazel to be embarrassed, she was, at that moment, embarrassed. Charlotte lowered her gaze.

"Wickliffe," she said in a small, troubled voice, "we were terribly worried about you. It has been so long since we heard. You knew about John. Wickliffe, Callam was killed, too, at Resaca. Last month. He was on General Hardee's staff." Mrs. Hazel sat erect and calm in stiff black silk. "Mason, I consider, has been the most unfortunate of my three sons," she said. "John and Callam lost their lives in battle, defending their honor and their land; Mason has had to stay at home—among the Yankees and women—and be a farmer."

That subject, it was clear, was distasteful to Mason Hazel. "You have told us nothing about yourself," he reminded Wickliffe.

"It is not very encouraging," he replied. "As usual, General Morgan is trying to create a diversion without either men or ammunition. We were a long while, after Morgan was captured in Ohio, getting down South again. That was a strange raid. A nightmare. We rode all day and all night. Always. We fought, I am certain, in our sleep. At Salem, Indiana, there was a toy cannon; it wasn't eighteen inches long, loaded to the muzzle, waiting for us in the public square. But no one was left to fire it. There was some pillaging—the provost guard tried its best to stop it—the most ridiculous pillaging you ever heard of. The town, it seemed, manufactured calico principally, and the men went off with bolts of it tied to their saddles. They would throw away one color and pick up another. A man in my company carried a bird cage with three canaries in it for two days. I had to make another throw away a useless chafing dish. A private, Mason, had seven pairs of skates hung around his neck. Then, at Piketon, a man broke through the guard posted at a store and filled his pockets with horn buttons. At Vienna, Colonel Smith made a feint against Madison. He returned the following morning.

"Vernon was next; it was held by a strong force, and we had to avoid Vernon. It was better at Dupont—they had a large meat-packing place, and when we left, every man had a ham slung at his saddle. But there was plenty to eat. The people baked once a week, they were always out when we stopped—there were stories about us, of course—and we got great quantities of bread. Hundreds of pies. We were blamed for not taking Cincinnati. Well, we couldn't take it. We couldn't have held it twenty-four hours if we had. Morgan didn't want Cincinnati. You see, we were trying to get away, to get home, then. Our purpose was almost accomplished. The old purpose—to create a diversion without men or ammunition. By then we were too tired, too exhausted, to think. I tell you we were twenty-two hours in the saddle day after day. Anyhow, we got lost going around Cincinnati at night. Cluke couldn't hold his regiment together—he never did except in battle; it was at the rear of the second brigade and strayed all over the country, so there was a long space between it and the first brigade. When we came to street crossings in the suburbs, part of the command would go one way and part another. It was so black and confusing, we had to light bundles of paper to find our way.

"Whenever we halted, everyone was asleep in a second. The men would go off into the fields and sleep until the enemy waked them up. We got away, at last, from Cincinnati. It began to look as though we were safe. As though we had been successful. At Williamsburg, General Morgan camped for the night. The next day we marched through a lot of towns and had a skirmish at Berlin. Nothing. Then we camped until three o'clock in the morning. By that time we had to chop our way through the trees felled across the road. All the bridges were burned. This was in July. On the eighteenth we stopped for an hour at Chester to re-form the column and find a guide. That was a mistake. It was fatal. We couldn't, then, reach the ford at Buffington, cross the Ohio, before dark. We got to the river bank about eight o'clock. There was an earthworks guarding the ford, and General Morgan couldn't make up his mind about attacking it. The position was defended by regular troops and they had two heavy guns. The column had to cross the river that night or never. It turned out to be never. The weather ruined us. Rain. The river was so high transports and gunboats came all the way up to Buffington Island. The ammunition for our artillery was done; there were less than three cartridges to the piece; it was pitch black, and we knew nothing about the land or the disposition of the enemy. We had to cross and we couldn't, with our force, assault an unknown position at night.

"General Morgan decided to attack at early dawn, and when it began to be light we moved against the fortification and found it empty. The force had gone away in the darkness. If our scouts had seen that, if they had been awake, almost the whole division would have been over the river before the Union troops arrived. Their advance guard came up and Colonel Smith smashed it. He took fifty prisoners and a piece of artillery. But General Judah was close behind with eight thousand men. We were in a valley that ran beside the Ohio for perhaps a mile, and very narrow at the south end. Colonel Smith formed there. He turned back Judah's cavalry, but it was no use. His two regiments didn't have five hundred men in them. General Hobson's force soon came up and joined Judah. We were between them, with the gunboats shelling us from the river.

"The valley was turned into a section of hell. Men in a panic were galloping every direction, trying to escape. Some still held on to their bolts of calico. The wagon train was a dreadful confusion of wild horses and howitzers. I was with the Sixth Kentucky regiment. We stood firm until General Morgan was out of the valley, and after that anything more was useless. We held back the Yankee cavalry until the gunboats raked us with grape, and then the men broke ranks. I swam the river and all but collided with a gunboat. General Morgan surrendered to a captain of militia; the captain granted him the most honorable terms, but General Shackelford refused to allow them."

A complete silence followed Wickliffe Sash's recital of the disaster to General Morgan's column in Ohio. His gaze fastened upon Charlotte. She was even lovelier, more desirable, than he had remembered. Charlotte looked up at him; an uncertain smile touched her lips, but even in the dim light he could see that her eyes were troubled.

"You must have something to eat," Mrs. Hazel said. She got up. "I will see what there is. Ham, probably, and cold chicken. Tomato preserves. Whisky would be better for you than Madeira."

Mason said, "I will get that. It is locked up. Hidden."

At last Wickliffe was alone with Charlotte Hazel. He went up to her and stood with his hands on her shoulders. She raised her head, and he realized that the trouble in her eyes, in her bearing, had deepened. Wickliffe disregarded that and caught her up, kissing her forehead and mouth. She was completely unresponsive; her face was bright with tears.

"Wait, Wickliffe," she half cried; "you must listen to me. When you do you won't want to be near me at all. You will hate me."

He stood back and regarded her with a questioning frown. He couldn't imagine what she was talking about. Wickliffe could not think what had come over Charlotte.

"Don't stare at me like that," she begged him. "Wickliffe, won't you sit down? It will make things easier. I have a lot to explain. You won't understand me, but I must go on just the same."

Wickliffe Sash brought a chair up to the sofa; he sat on it, grave and attentive. "She hates my beard," he told himself. "I was an idiot not to have it cut off in Lexington."

"Wickliffe," she began, "I am a bad girl. My heart is bad. Do you remember how we felt about people who went with the North—who deserted their land and people? Well, I am worse than that. I have deserted my land. I haven't been faithful to my people. If you had been here, perhaps it wouldn't have happened. I don't know about that. No one could, could they? Mother says it should not have happened because you weren't here. She says I failed in the simplest obligation of honor. Wickliffe, my mother will never have anything to do with me again. Not really. Compared with me, John and Callam are both alive at Greenland. I am dead, and not they. Mason is a little better—at least he has been kind to me." She leaned forward desperately.

"Wickliffe, do you remember where we were when I first realized you loved me? Of course you do. It was at Mrs. Abel's, in Frankfort. The party just before the war started in Kentucky. You all rushed off to Lexington, to capture the Lincoln guns or keep them from being captured. It depended on whether you were for the North or the South. We walked away from everyone. Down to the river. Do you remember the roses and how the frogs croaked at us? Croaking frogs." Yes, he told her, it was all clear in his memory. Charlotte went on: "I was thirteen then. Thirteen, and I said I would love you all my life. I promised I would marry you when you came back from the war. Thirteen, Wickliffe. Won't you help me and admit that is very young for promises? Especially promises of love."

"I never thought of it as either young or old," he replied. "I loved you and wanted you, and I knew I would always want you. I said to myself,'When the time comes we'll be married.' That is all I thought. Naturally, it couldn't happen then. By the river." He was filled with a mingled dread and impatience. "Perhaps you had better make this clearer," he added. "There is a good deal of it I don't understand."

Charlotte drew in a long breath and for a moment shut her eyes. "Wickliffe, I can't marry you," she said at last. "I can't, and the reason is I love someone else."

A profound silence closed about them in the thinly lighted formal room. Wickliffe's impatience vanished; it was dissolved in a sudden pain like a blow at his heart. Her words echoed in his mind—"Wickliffe, I can't marry you." She could not marry him because she loved someone else. An angry resentment, the voice of his damaged masculine pride, spoke first:

"How did you find out you loved someone else?" he demanded. "Didn't whoever it was know you were going to marry me?" Most of that, however, Wickliffe realized, she would not answer. Whoever it was she now loved must do that.

"I don't know!" she exclaimed. "I can't tell you how any of it happened. I have to go on. It's Isham Rose; that won't mean anything to you. He was born in Irvine but he has been living in the North, and he is a captain in the Forty-fifth Kentucky regiment. You see, it couldn't be worse for any of us."

"That is Colonel Brown's brigade," Wickliffe said mechanically. "It is in the east now, with Burbridge's division, trying to destroy Morgan."

"Yes," Charlotte Hazel replied, "Isham is in the mountains. Somewhere between Louisa and Pound Gap. Do we have to talk about that? There is so much else nearer to us. Anyhow, the regiment was in Irvine in April; Isham joined it there, and then he was moved to Lexington. I met him at Green New's house. I loved him right away, Wickliffe. In a second. I wanted him to love me then. The first time we saw each other, at Green's. You have to understand that. How bad I was. It's the only excuse I could make. I mean the way it happened. I didn't stop to think. I couldn't. I didn't want to. I only wanted Isham. Wickliffe, I have to say it this way! Darling, you must hate me. If it had dragged on it couldn't have happened. Then I would have been worse than I am. If possible. I asked Isham to come to Greenland, in spite of what mother would think and what Mason might say. Mother, naturally, refused to come down. To meet him at all. We stood on the porch, and, all at once, it was over. I had promised to marry you, and I told Isham Rose he could have me whenever he wanted."

Wickliffe Sash, his eyes narrowed, gazed with a steady curiosity at Charlotte. She was lovelier by far than he had remembered. Lovelier and false. She had, engaged to marry him, offered herself—no, thrown herself at another man. A

Kentuckian fighting in a Union regiment against his own traditions and blood. A Kentuckian occupied at that moment in hunting down General Morgan. He forgot that, thinking more particularly of Charlotte and himself. Wickliffe wanted her more than ever, the pain at his heart was unbearable, and at the same time he completely realized that he would never possess her. Not now. He wanted her more than ever, and yet he couldn't have her. Charlotte, who was so lovely, was a liar. She had betrayed him.

He repeated, "Did this Captain Rose know you were engaged to me? That, I think, is important." It wasn't, he realized, it couldn't be, important to Charlotte now. She would say anything to protect Isham Rose. Her answer was what he expected.

"I saw him at Green New's almost the first day he was in Lexington," she replied; "he hadn't met anyone we know until then, and he came to Greenland the next afternoon. Wickliffe, he couldn't have heard about us. I told him myself, later."

"What did he say?" Wickliffe Sash asked.

"Isham said he was sorry, but it could not be helped. He would, he said, accept all the responsibilities of marrying me. I do know this, Wickliffe, he wants to see you."

Wickliffe replied, "Naturally. He is with General Burbridge. They want to see everyone in Morgan's command. I don't imagine he will until later. Perhaps in Virginia. Captain Rose is still hunting for us near Pound Gap."

He felt suddenly older by a very great deal. In a few minutes. In no time at all, his life, all life, had grown darker, less desirable. Some more of its security had gone forever. This, he realized, in the terms of battle, was a serious wound. He would not recover from it. Wickliffe's pride, his sense of Charlotte's great failure, held his feelings resolutely checked. He was at least able to conduct himself with an appropriate dignity.

"There isn't much I can say," he proceeded in a steady and cold voice. "You are quite released from your obligation to me. I asked a question about Captain Rose and I must accept your answer. That, I think, is the end of my responsibility where he is concerned. It hasn't appeared that he acted dishonorably." He fell abruptly silent.

"I understand, Wickliffe," Charlotte said; "I am dishonorable and you are glad to know it now. Before it is too late."

He could see that Charlotte was immensely relieved. She was entirely free now to love and marry Isham Rose—Captain Rose of the Forty-fifth Kentucky regiment in the Federal Army. He saw, too, that nothing else was important to her. Nothing he said, nothing her mother said, could reach or affect her. Charlotte's love shut everything else out from her. She was supremely indifferent to the rest of the world. It made her very hard, wholly unsympathetic. Charlotte was sorry for him, Wickliffe Sash, but no more. Mrs. Hazel came into the room and glanced rapidly from her daughter to him. She said nothing, however, except that some things were ready in the dining room. Mrs. Hazel did add that Mason would sit with him; he wanted to hear all that Wickliffe knew about their army and the Confederacy. She had not finished speaking when there was a rapid passage of feet in the hall. A tall young man, without a beard, clad in the blue uniform of the Union Army, stood in the doorway. He spoke at once to Charlotte, overlooking the others.

"If it was wrong to appear so informally, I am sorry," he told her. "I couldn't find any servants. Charlotte, I have no time at all, but I had to see you for a moment. General Burbridge is here. Rather, he'll be here any time now. The troops at Louisville have been notified. Morgan didn't expect us for days—" He stopped abruptly, at last conscious of Wickliffe Sash. Wickliffe moved forward with his revolver held point-blank on the blue coat before him.

"I suppose you are Captain Rose," he said.

"Yes, I am Isham Rose," Rose replied. "You must be Wickliffe Sash." He was entirely cool. Apparently no revolver was in sight.

"I am interested in what you just told Charlotte," Wickliffe proceeded; "of course it is all a lie. Perhaps you had better sit down. On that chair by the wall. Sit down and fold your arms. Anything else would be a serious mistake." Isham Rose deliberately followed Wickliffe's directions. "General Burbridge," Wickliffe asserted, "won't be here, he can't be, for two or three days more."

"I am not in the habit of lying or waving revolvers before women," Rose answered. "You think no one but Morgan can make forced marches. Morgan thought that, apparently, and it will finish him. It might interest you, a cavalryman, to hear that we marched ninety miles in less than thirty hours. With artillery. You didn't reckon on that. It didn't occur to General Morgan that we would be in Mount Sterling as soon as he was."

"That is a lie," Wickliffe repeated. A feeling of dread settled over him. Rose, he knew, had been completely truthful. Burbridge was in the bluegrass, General Morgan did not know it, and the result of that ignorance, of his mistake, might very well be fatal.

This was the night of the eighth. Morgan had planned to be in Lexington late on the ninth or, at worst, very early of the next day. He was moving west as rapidly as possible now. Burbridge, it was probable, hadn't come up with him yet. General Morgan must be informed of the Federal approach at once.

"How long will it be necessary for me to sit here?" Rose asked him.

Wickliffe, the truth was, did not know. He had to leave immediately, and that necessity, complicated with the presence of Isham Rose, presented certain difficulties. Rose, he could see, would not agree to a peaceable departure. Captain Rose had as much interest in delaying him as he had in hurrying away to warn his commander. Wickliffe gazed doubtfully at Charlotte and Mrs. Hazel. Charlotte had sunk back on the sofa where she had been sitting; her hands were tightly clasped; her face was pinched with terror. Mrs. Hazel was standing, pale and composed. It was a desperate situation for all of them. Wickliffe said to himself, "I will have to kill him. I must get off. There is no other way to do that." He couldn't, he discovered, coldly shoot Isham Rose before Charlotte and her mother. Mason Hazel came into the room. He had stopped between Wickliffe and Rose, and he quickly moved aside.

"Mason," Wickliffe Sash said, "I want you to take Charlotte and your mother away. They had better go upstairs. Something very painful has happened."

Mason Hazel went up to his mother and gently took her arm. "Come, mother," he addressed her; "Charlotte, I want you to be with her. Please." Charlotte stood up insecurely.

"Before you go," Isham Rose interrupted them, "I ought to explain a difficulty in this situation. Captain Sash, who has thought of nothing but his duty, has missed it. I am not, I hope you will realize, speaking for myself. It is clear Sash intends to kill me. That is proper. At the same time—and my orderly is outside with the horses—if I am shot to death here, in Greenland, the provost marshal's guard will burn down the house. They will retaliate on Mr. Hazel and send Mrs. Hazel and Charlotte to prisons in the North. If they are fortunate. I want to prevent that, if it's possible."

All Rose had said was, Wickliffe Sash saw again, clearly true. If, as he would be forced to do, he left Rose shot at Greenland, an example would be made of the Hazels that even in imagination he could not face.

Mrs. Hazel spoke in a firm voice: "You cannot listen to him, Wickliffe. General Morgan must be reached. We are of no importance here. Not compared with that. John and Callam have met their responsibility, and Mason won't hesitate. Charlotte and I will contrive to live through it."

Charlotte rose with an exclamation of protest. Wickliffe was afraid that, in her panic, she would throw herself upon him; Mason caught her arm. He held her with an arm about her waist.

"Come, Charlotte," Mrs. Hazel said with immense dignity. "We will leave the gentlemen."

They went, Charlotte still restrained by her brother, leaving Wickliffe faced with his regrettable situation.

"You will be too late," Isham Rose warned him. "Burbridge will overtake your column tonight. Greenland will be sacrificed for nothing."

Wickliffe Sash made no immediate answer. He ought to kill Rose where he sat, without a moment's hesitation, and get away. That was his duty. He was, he found, unable to follow it. His revolver was pointed directly and steadily at Isham Rose. He could not force himself to pull the trigger. The provost marshal might very easily hang all three of the Hazels—Charlotte and Mrs. Hazel and Mason. He might shoot Rose and then, with luck, kill the orderly and leave them for Mason to dispose of. Mason could hide the bodies in an old well; there was a chance they would not be found. He might even drive the horses off into the night.

It was too dangerous, he decided; there were still servants, negroes, in the place, and they would hear the shots. It was even possible to kill Rose and the orderly with the heavy knife Wickliffe carried at his belt. The question of the blood occurred to him. A man, Wickliffe well knew, held an amazing lot of it. No, Mason Hazel, alone, could not accomplish so much before light. There was one other, a last possibility.

"I understand," he proceeded, "that you are engaged to Charlotte Hazel. When that occurred she was promised to me. Charlotte told me that you acted innocently. You didn't know she was not free. I believed her then, but now, since I have seen you, I'm not so sure about it. In other words, there may be the material of a difference between us. I am inclined to think you have done me a serious wrong."

"I wondered if that would come up," Isham Rose replied. "It is very reasonable. If you will agree to it, I'll write a note we can both sign and give it to the orderly. I will explain the circumstances to him and let him attend me, and Mason can stand with you."

Wickliffe put his pistol back in its holster. "Thank you," he said simply. Mason returned to the drawing-room. "Captain Rose and myself have arranged a meeting," Wickliffe explained. "He wishes to write a note first."

Mason took Isham Rose across the hall to a desk. An overwhelming realization took possession of Wickliffe—he had no right to risk his life in a duel. He had, now, no private or personal honor. Only one thing was important, and that was the danger concentrating about General Morgan. He went quickly to a long side window, open upon the lawn, and dropped lightly into the night outside. Wickliffe Sash quickly and noiselessly unfastened his horse from the rack by the slave quarters.

The ugly black horse, he discovered, galloping through the night, had an extraordinary measure of endurance. The animal showed hardly a sign of weariness. Wickliffe didn't know how far he would be forced to ride—General Morgan was at Mount Sterling, the troops stationed there would create no serious difficulty, and when the town was taken he would move with the greatest possible rapidity toward Lexington.

Probably he'd encounter the column between Aaron's Run and Stoner Creek. He could not believe that Burbridge had overtaken General Morgan. "Probably," Wickliffe told himself, "that will happen tomorrow and there will be a battle. Morgan will attack where the Federal line is weakest and escape again." He had always escaped, Wickliffe realized. The Yankees could never hold General Morgan. His thoughts returned to Greenland, to Charlotte and Isham Rose. His love for Charlotte was dead. That part of him was dead. Charlotte Hazel had been unfaithful. Not so much to him as to herself. Charlotte had broken her word.

In a wholly different sense he had broken his word to Captain Rose. He had agreed to meet Rose in a duel and then run away. He wondered uncomfortably what Rose said, what Mrs. Hazel thought, when they discovered he had gone? Charlotte would be relieved. There was, however, no doubt in Wickliffe Sash's mind about the propriety of his course. It didn't matter what anyone thought of him. "If I do see Rose later," he told himself, "I can offer him all the satisfaction he will require." Isham Rose, the truth was, had behaved very well indeed; he was almost contemptuous in his courage. His attitude toward Greenland had been admirable—Wickliffe could see that Isham Rose was a good soldier. "I hope I meet him again," he proceeded. "I owe him something."

Earlier memories of Charlotte and his family filled his mind—he had never loved, he had never thought, of another girl. It had begun when he was eighteen and Charlotte nine. They had, he considered, always belonged to each other. Now she was gone, his life seemed strange and empty. Without, except for the South, any purpose. It would be stranger, emptier, when the war was over. It must be over some day. The South would lose everything. No, a miracle— General Lee—would save it. Europe would come to the assistance of the Confederacy. The North must grow tired of pouring men and supplies into the consuming flames of Southern resistance. There was a faint trace of morning in the east, trees and fences were easily visible, there were lights in farmhouse windows. A sudden freshness was perceptible, a delightful fragrant coolness touched Wickliffe Sash's cheeks. The east was rose-colored, the zenith tenderly azure. The grass sparkled with crystal dew. The morning was innocent and pure, gay with flowers and musical with little pastoral sounds; lambs were white on the blue-green meadows, and a colt was gracefully clumsy.

A feeling of melancholy, of longing for old tranquillity, possessed Wickliffe. He wanted to be very young again, shooting gray squirrels in the woods of Calydon on a morning exactly like this. Lost in thought, in memories, he rode directly into the forward vedettes of General Morgan's column. "Burbridge is in the bluegrass," he informed them, hurrying by. It seemed to Wickliffe Sash that he was followed by a scoffing and weary laugh. He pulled the horse up sharply and delivered his intelligence to General Morgan.

The general thanked him: "I am indebted to you, Captain Sash. I can see you have ridden hard. You have done well. We haven't been so fortunate."

Wickliffe Sash asked, "Shall I transmit any orders concerning General Burbridge's advanced position to my battalion?"

"Unfortunately, that is not necessary," Morgan replied; "they know it already."

Wickliffe saluted and dropped to the rear of the column. He was too late.

"Where is Lieutenant Brenno?" he asked a man riding at the head of some men familiar to him.

"He is dead, sir," the man replied.

"Why isn't Mr. Liman at the company head?" Wickliffe continued.

"Mr. Liman is dead too," he was informed. "Sergeant Shuck is killed, and Thomas Haskins and Moses Henry. All the sergeants. And Ambrose Huffman. I am Corporal Martin Grider. We were cut to pieces last night, just before three o'clock, holding the rear guard."

Wickliffe joined the officers riding with Colonel Martin at the head of the brigade. Martin's head was bandaged and the wrapping was bright with fresh blood; he was grimly silent; he would speak, Wickliffe saw, to no one. Lieutenant Colonel Brent, however, was talking continuously, in a tone of suppressed resentment, to Major Diamond.

"No one knew Burbridge was in a hundred miles of us," he protested. "General Morgan had no idea of it. Colonel

Martin went regularly to bed in a house back from the command. There wasn't a word of danger from our direction. Not a whisper of it, or a thought. I sent my picket out, according to orders, and had guards along the road."

Major Diamond nodded shortly and unsympathetically; he left Brent and rode beside Wickliffe Sash.

"George," Wickliffe demanded, "tell me what happened. I found out, in Lexington, that Burbridge was close behind us. I rode all night, on a horse that had wings, but it seems without accomplishing anything."

Major Diamond was bitter. "Brent swears he sent a picket far enough down the road. He didn't. I heard Colonel Martin tell him to post a guard a mile back of the camp. I doubt if it was a hundred yards away. He had between forty and fifty men of our first battalion on rear-guard duty. Well, Burbridge surprised them. The Federal cavalry was in the camp before anyone, hardly, was awake; they shot the men and cut them down lying around their fires. Wickliffe, they never had a chance. Martin was sleeping in a farmhouse and he rode through the whole Union force to reach his command. By that time the Yankees had occupied Mount Sterling again—we had captured it once—and when we were forced to retreat we had to cut our way through the town. You know what that is like—muskets in every window and guns with grape at the cross streets.

"We got through that and met Giltner about two miles farther on; Martin persuaded him to go back and attack again; and it was agreed for Giltner to advance on the front of Mount Sterling while Martin assaulted in the rear. It turned out to be another of those damned occasions when we ran out of cartridges. A draw. We withdrew and the Federal troops were so badly shot up they couldn't follow us. We lost fourteen commissioned officers and forty men, eighty were left badly wounded in Mount Sterling, a hundred more were captured." Wickliffe was silent; it was evident that General Morgan had suffered a serious, perhaps a fatal, defeat. "This time," Diamond asserted, "we are finished. At last. Morgan's column. Most of us now, Wickliffe, will stay in Kentucky. Where we were born. Where we belong. The bluegrass. We won't care if the Yankees own it or not. State rights and the negroes won't bother us. The dark and bloody ground is bloody and dark again. Worse than ever. I suppose peace will come to Kentucky some day, after us; we have had nothing but war so far."

"I wouldn't know what to do if the world turned peaceful," Wickliffe Sash admitted. "It seems to me I've been riding in column, mounted and on foot, forever. Fighting and retreating. The retreat a little harder every time. Before that, all my life, this war was kept up. Political or actually. If I did go home, it wouldn't be there. Not with everyone I knew and cared for pretty well killed. My brothers are dead; my father will never recover from a saber cut, my mother, who was so gay and young, is an old woman. My cousins, who were children with me, have murdered one another by now. Elisha Abel is missing. All three of the News are dead. Callam and John Hazel are gone, and Charlotte is gone too."

He didn't continue. Wickliffe rode with his head down, a snaffle rein loose in his hand.

The column came in sight of Lexington; there was a slight engagement, scattered shots from sheltered positions, and General Morgan rode into the city. Wickliffe helped to burn the Union depot and stables, he shifted his saddle to a fresh horse, and had a bath at the Phoenix Hotel. What was left of the third brigade—the men were all mounted now—was consolidated with their original battalions in the first and second. The command hurried on toward Georgetown; Wickliffe Sash was detached in a demonstration against Frankfort.

He was, so far as it could be discovered, successful; his detail rode again all night and overtook the main body outside Cynthiana. Wickliffe's position was irregular, he had no company; he served as temporary aide to Colonel Martin. There was little time for rigid military alignment. It was the eleventh of June. A sharp fight followed around the Union garrison; after an hour it surrendered; Wickliffe, who had charge of the prisoners, roughly counted four hundred Federal soldiers. He paroled them upon his own responsibility, and then he was occupied with a squad of men attempting to put out a fire that had started among the small frame dwellings of the town. General Morgan stopped to direct him. He was, Wickliffe recognized, in a state of suppressed anger. Morgan was especially sharp about all damage or losses that might be blamed on his troops. He bitterly resented the charges in the Union papers that he was no better than a partisan raider who carried destruction into his own state.

The fight had scarcely stopped in Cynthiana when there was a renewed rattle of shots on the outskirts—a supporting force of Union cavalry under General Hobson had arrived. Morgan, attended by Wickliffe Sash, detached Major Cassel's battalion from the occupation of the fortifications, attacking Hobson in the rear. Wickliffe's horse was shot in the muzzle and became unmanageable. He was half thrown to the ground and shot a Federal officer in the face who was riding over him. He was kicked by a horse—lightly, it was fortunate, but his left trouser was torn off to his boot. A constant rill of blood ran down that leg. There was a sharp blow at his shoulder; it whirled him about; he had been shot; an arm hung useless at his side. A glitter of steel, a saber swept by his eyes. It was the first thing, Wickliffe thought, that had missed him. He caught a Union major by the belt and dragged him down; the major clubbed him on the head with his pistol butt. One, two crashing blows. Wickliffe drove his knife into the officer's back.

They fell together. Wickliffe Sash lost consciousness; he came to almost at once and found that General Hobson had been captured and his cavalry routed. He walked, swaying, toward Colonel Giltner, and an orderly gave him a horse. The orderly wiped the blood out of Wickliffe's eyes and helped him into the saddle. General Morgan had left and a bugle blew urgently for assembly in Cynthiana. Wickliffe Sash awkwardly loaded his revolver with one hand; he held it with his knee against the saddle. His head hurt outrageously and there was a grinding pain in his hip, but the wound in his shoulder didn't bother him.

Giltner said, "Captain Sash, I believe you are almost home. It is folly for you to stay with the column. Will you accept my order to leave the field?"

"Thank you, Colonel Giltner," Wickliffe replied. He continued to ride beside his superior. Nothing more was said about his retirement from action. They came upon General Morgan in the center of the town. The Confederates were emptying the military depot and destroying the stores. General Hobson was mounted at Morgan's side. He left shortly, under the escort of General Morgan and two other officers, for Cincinnati. Wickliffe sat on the edge of a porch.

The house was deserted. It was very hot. His head had stopped bleeding, but the pain continued. It increased. He didn't see how it could, but it did. He ought to see a surgeon. The effort to move, either to walk or ride, was more than he could undertake. Instead he was actively sick. Then he fell asleep. When Wickliffe woke up, the dusk had gathered in Cynthiana. He was hungry, and hobbled into the house, where he found the end of a ham and a kettle of vegetable soup. It would be splendid to have some bread, he thought. Bread, bread, bread, he repeated, looking for it. There was none. He consumed the cold soup.

Waves of increasing weakness swept over him. He lay down on a hard couch and slept and woke up, slept and woke up. Something was broken in his hip. Wickliffe had to lie on the other side, and that made it necessary for him to change the position of his revolver. An enormous undertaking. He would get up in a little and rejoin his command. General Morgan would move westward very early in the morning. A battle set up between his will and his injured body. "I must go back to the column," he told himself; intolerable pain threatened to defeat that resolution. At last he forced himself to move. Wickliffe sat up and then slowly made his way to the porch. His horse was tied to a porch pillar. He walked beside the animal, holding on to the rein and the saddle. The morning once more opened like the petals of a flower, a rose, about him. Wickliffe told himself that he felt better. He managed, at a mounting block, to get on his horse.

The two brigades were gathering in the center of town. General Morgan addressed their staffs. "We have less than twelve hundred available men," he asserted. "The rest, who are not killed, are guarding prisoners and on the wagon train. Two details are still tearing up the tracks of the Kentucky Central Railroad. We will retreat at once. Rapid as possible. By the Augusta road. The entire command will move in column, with a mounted reserve to cover the rear."

Disaster immediately followed. Giltner was cut off and forced to retreat toward Leesburg. He made an effort to form his men, against an overwhelming force, in line of battle.

"Where is Colonel Smith?" he cried at Wickliffe.

Lieutenant Andrews, attached to Smith, rode up to them. "We will be here at once!" he shouted above the volleying of Enfield rifles.

Colonel Smith's brigade arrived; it drove the Union advance back, but a massed attack broke through Colonel Bowles' position.

"It's over now," Wickliffe Sash told himself. He was behind a stone wall, dismounted, with what remained of Bowles' forces.

They were driven from that cover. Wickliffe saw Major Kirkpatrick carried from the field. He retreated slowly, with Smith's command, toward Cynthiana, and found that they were surrounded by Burbridge's army, with the Licking River at one side. Colonel Smith led his men through the river; they met a body of cavalry on the opposite bank, and scattering it, they vanished from Wickliffe Sash's view. He couldn't mount. He was helpless to follow them. Well, the war, for him, was done. He walked and rested, leaned against trees or fences or walls. Every time he stopped, it was more difficult to walk. Federal soldiers rode by, ignoring him. He scarcely moved out of the horses' way. An officer approached him more slowly. He stopped.

"I am glad it is you," Wickliffe said.

It was Captain Isham Rose. He dismounted. "Let me help you," Rose said.

"No," Wickliffe Sash replied.

"Don't be stubborn," Captain Rose begged him; "you are badly hurt."

Wickliffe repeated, "No, it is nothing. I am in your debt."

The question of debt, Isham Rose told him, they could settle later.

"No," Wickliffe said.

They stood by a house with a side yard where the wall was bright with tall hollyhocks flowering in the sun. The air was sweet with the perfume of cinnamon roses.

"My right hand is still good," he asserted. He walked back into the side yard, followed by the man Charlotte Hazel had planned to marry.

"I protest against all of this," Rose insisted.

Wickliffe Sash said, "I challenged you originally. Are you satisfied with navy revolver at ten paces?" They took their positions on a narrow walk of planks. "Will you agree to turn and fire?" Wickliffe further asked. Isham Rose replied that he would agree to turn and fire. Wickliffe stood with his back to him. The side yard ended in a high fence that badly needed paint. "Turn!" he cried. He wheeled and let drop his revolver. There was a stunning sound like a bolt of thunder. The sun vanished in a pall of blackness.

He heard, very far away, a voice.

"In God's name," it begged him, "why did you hold your fire?"

He replied thinly out of the changing elements of dissolution: "I ran from my privilege to it."

The darkness rolled back: Wickliffe Sash was in the bluegrass, a wide pastoral land where horses grazed slowly with flowing manes and tails, and red Devon cattle, burnished by the sun, were like animals in copper. The woodland pastures were cool and gracious with shade. The great doors at Calydon stood open. His brothers called to him in their play. Nothingness gently enfolded him.

The Bloodhounds

W.C. MORROW

In 1864 the horrors of war spread over the South like a pall of death. Not only did they stalk among the soldiers to strip the rags from their backs; to starve them or to feed them on rotten meat; to place them in the deadly path of the Minie or the murderous grape; to mow them down with foul disease and loathsome suffering; but they sent conscription, to feed mothers on despair and children on stones, and hunger to take up its abode at the fireside of the poor. The facilities of the transitory and feeble government for supplying means of sustenance to poor families were inadequate in remote and sparsely settled communities; and now that the husband, on whom had depended the livelihood of his family, had been armed with a musket and ordered to the front, there was no lack of anguish and the distressing cry of children for bread. The despairing mother wrote to her husband on paper that was blotted with tears, and from every word there stared at him the suffering faces of his children and the imploring look that no parent can withstand. So the stanch soldier, who could unflinchingly storm a rampart or face a cannon, and who looked upon death as his companion and honor as his future shroud, employed his affections as his gravedigger, and sneaked away in the darkness like a thief. Desertion and death were synonymous terms, and the man sacrificed his life to feed his children. Depletion of the ranks by desertion assumed such alarming proportions that the War Department stretched forth its relentless arm and stained its sword with the blood of its own men. It was not a question of bread for children, but of men for the vanguard. Desertion was, in point of numbers, equivalent to death on the battlefield, so far as it affected the strength of the line; in point of discipline it was a thousand times worse. A man's life was worth nothing unless it served to check the career of a rifle ball directed at the vitals of the government. To such a desperate strait had the war policy of the Confederate Government been reduced that, in order to discourage a defection that was becoming epidemic, a patrol was employed, which, with the assistance of hounds in rare instances, hunted the deserters down and hanged them in chains, or shot them, blindfolded, with their faces to the wall.

One day a deserter named Martin was at work in a cornfield attached to his humble dwelling. Four or five pale, ragged, emaciated children were amusing themselves in the yard, and a homely, care-worn woman was bending over a washtub, while her infant, with hollowed eyes and wasted limbs, was playing in the dirt at her side. The man had been at home unmolested for two months, and had come to experience a faint sense of security. When darkness came on he shouldered his hoe and trudged to the house, taking in his arms a few pine knots which were to furnish light for the evening. The family sat down to a supper of corn bread, which they washed down with a disgusting drink, too familiar in those days to nearly all classes, and especially to those on whom the hunger of war pressed most heavily. It was made from corn, roasted until it was black; it was called "coffee," and was drunk without sugar.

"Well, Mary," said the husband, "the corn will be in roasting ear in two weeks, and we will have something fit to eat."

"Yes," said the woman.

"And then, you know, the birds will begin to flock in, and I can trap a few of them and get meat."

"Yes."

"I think we're going to get along first rate. I don't believe the war will last three months longer. You know one reason for so much desertion is that a great many soldiers have no idea now that we can ever whip the North, and they think that if they desert the Confederacy will go under before the patrol can catch them. I'm thinking that I am almost out of danger."

"I hope so, William; but there's no telling."

"All right, Mary; but they can't take me alive."

This declaration was made with such a calm and quiet determination that the poor woman looked anxiously at the hard lines about his eyes and mouth. She knew that he meant it, and that the loaded revolver he always carried would never hesitate a moment.

In striking contrast to the woman, the man was of powerful build. His hardships in the army had toughened his muscles and strengthened his large bones and supple joints. In a simple measure of strength he would have been a match for two ordinary men. His shoulders were broad and erect, and his arms and legs large and full of power.

They sat silently watching the blazing knots in the broad fireplace, the woman wearily engaged with some coarse knitting and the man smoking home made tobacco in an old clay pipe. On a sudden the man took the pipe from his mouth, straightened his shoulders, and listened attentively. His wife noticed the movement, and hurriedly whispered:

"What is it, William?"

"Sh-h-h."

They listened a moment longer, and the man stealthily rose to his feet and gazed steadily at the door, which was barred on the inside.

"What is it, William?" the woman again whispered, having strained her hearing in vain to catch any unusual sound.

"Horses."

"Where?"

He answered by pointing in the direction of the road. The truth flashed upon the woman's mind that, beyond a doubt, a hunting party was abroad, and that their game was a deserter. She rose to her feet, very pale, and regarded her husband with an anxious look. The man glanced at his children, lying asleep on their cots, cast a loving look at his wife, stepped softly to a shelf on which was a bucket of water, and dashed its contents upon the fire. The blaze was extinguished, and the room was in profound darkness.

"Run, William!" whispered the woman in a quavering voice.

He silently clasped her in his arms, and said: "Keep a brave heart, Mary. They can't take me alive."

He pushed her away, although she unconsciously clung to him, pulled out his revolver, cocked it, and let the hammer down softly. He then put on his hat, quietly unbarred the door, and slipped out in the dark.

The sound of the horses' hoofs had ceased. The woman staggered to the open door, and saw several dark forms hurrying around the cottage. They must have seen her husband, for a stern voice called "Halt!" and she heard the click of a carbine. A shadowy figure stole crouching alongside a fence, and on hearing the command it suddenly straightened, and bounded forward like a frightened deer. There was a vivid flash and a report from the carbine, and the stealthy figure halted a moment, and returned the fire. The soldier fell as a pistol ball crashed through his shoulder; the fugitive ran with redoubled speed, and disappeared in the darkness. There was a rapid discharge of carbines, but Martin had gained the swamp, and further pursuit was out of the question.

The hunters returned and bore the wounded man into the woman's cottage. She rekindled the fire, and assisted with trembling hands in dressing the wound.

"How long has your husband been here?" asked the captain.

"Two months."

"Where will he go?"

"I don't know."

"You do know!"

The woman made no reply.

"Do you know you are guilty of harboring a deserter?"

"Yes," she said, firmly and proudly, looking him full in the face.

"Do you know what can be done with you?"

She said nothing.

"You can be arrested and punished for a crime."

She regarded him with intense scorn, and remained silent.

"I'm glad he got away," she said, at length, quietly.

"Did you assist him in escaping?"

"He needed no help."

"He surely told you where he was going?"

She shook her head.

"Did he say when he will come back?"

"No."

"Now, I see that you are a woman of sense and courage. If you will tell me where I can find him I will not arrest you."

She treated the proposition with contemptuous silence.

"You would not like to be handcuffed and carried to prison?"

"I wouldn't care."

"What would become of your children?"

The woman became pale, her eyes flashed, and she stammered:

"You would not leave them here to starve, would you?"

"Certainly," said the officer, as he laughed at her agony.

The mother was transformed into a tigress. She sprang across the room, seized a carbine that leaned against the wall, and leveled it at his head.

"You would! you cowardly, inhuman brute!" She screamed as she pulled the trigger.

There was a deafening report, and she fell fainting to the floor.

"Simply sheared me a little," remarked the officer, as with a certain degree of interest he felt a narrow white streak that the ball had cut through his hair. "'An inch lower, and'—what was it old Nap said at Austerlitz? She's game, though, and quick as lightning. No use trying to get anything out of her. I just wanted to scare her a little, and she took it in dead earnest."

"What are you going to do now, Captain?" asked one of the men.

"Oh, I'll put Walker's dogs after him. They'll fetch him."

"The Bloodhounds?"

"Yes."

"Will you follow them up?"

"I don't know."

"They'll never leave him alive if you don't."

"I know it."

"That would be terrible."

"Why?"

"They got that fellow, Rutherford, down, and tore him to pieces."

"Well, what's the difference? Is that any worse than calling the dogs off, and bringing him back alive to be shot?"

"But he's armed and will kill the hounds."

"Twelve dogs? Don't be uneasy. He will finish two or three of the younger dogs until his pistol is empty, and the rest will manage him. Old Tiger will be there at the finish, and will make all the final arrangements for the funeral. He hangs on closer than death, and they've never got a square blow nor a safe shot at him yet."

At daybreak the next morning an old man, smooth-shaved and stoop-shouldered, was riding in the direction of the woman's cottage. The cavalry captain accompanied him, and eleven bloodhounds—magnificent dogs—trotted along, some ahead and others on either side of the horsemen, while two hundred yards in the rear a solitary old dog jogged along as if already weary of the enterprise and disgusted with the life he was called upon to lead. This was none other than the famous Tiger, more generally called "Old Tige," the dog that never lost a trail, and never failed to run his game to earth.

"Walker," said the officer, "I think we had better skirt the woods, and not let the woman know that we've got the dogs out. She might give us trouble."

They entered the swamp in the direction the man had taken, and Walker called the dogs about him. Tiger walked leisurely up, and lay down near his master's horse.

"Heigho! get up, sir!"

The old dog slowly obeyed the command, and stood blinking and staring stupidly at his master. Walker descended from his horse, and pointing to the ground, said:

"Hie on!"

The other dogs were already scouring the ground in all directions. Old Tige put his nose to the grass, and began to hunt the scent, by systematically describing a circle which he continually widened, his master watching him closely the meanwhile, and paying no attention to the other dogs. A young hound soon sent up the well-known howl, and the other dogs chased eagerly around him, Old Tige trotting to the scene behind all the others. The dogs were greatly excited. The old dog unceremoniously pushed his way through the crowd, and sniffed the ground. The young hound, impatient that no command was given, and satisfied that he had found the trail, slowly advanced into the swamp, his nose all the time to the ground. Soon he set off on a full run, the other dogs following with yelps. Old Tige examined the spot indicated by the young hound, but was entirely unconcerned, and proceeded to smell the ground for a few yards around. Walker called the other dogs back, and Old Tige sullenly shook his head until his ragged ears flapped against his jowls, and lay down again.

"He's not satisfied," said Walker. "I will have to show him the track. He's in doubt."

Walker crept along the fence, followed by the old dog, and when he had reached the spot opposite where the man was last seen, he saw through the fence a track indented in the soft earth, and ordered the dog to climb over. Old Tige clambered laboriously over the rails, and scented the track. He regained his master's side, and trudged with him back to the swamp.

"I think the woman heard the dogs," said Walker. "I saw her looking through the door and listening. Tiger's got the scent. Hie away, sir!"

The dog hunted for a few moments, and found the trail. With a single yelp he disappeared in the thicker part of the underbrush, and the whole pack bounded yelping after him. They pursued the trail for a mile through the swamp, and mounted a hill on the opposite side. They disappeared over the summit, and Old Tige, already far behind, reached the highest point and came to a standstill. He remained for one or two minutes surveying the surrounding country, and then struck off at a right angle from the trail, with his nose high in the air and his tail straight with his back. He went in the direction of a large plateau covered with tall pines and salamander hills. Occasionally he would stop, as if listening to the yelping of the hounds as it rapidly grew fainter in the distance. Having traversed the plateau, which was five miles in width, he came to the outskirts of a canebrake, and bent his nose to the ground. He proceeded two miles along the edge of the dense growth of cane until he found a path which led through. The traveler would be compelled to pick his way through the mud and water by stepping carefully upon poles and cypress roots. The dog sniffed the ground attentively at the entrance to the swamp, and a sudden swishing of the tail and a loud snorting showed that he had found the trail. Before entering he looked behind him and listened for the dogs, standing the meanwhile on three legs and as still as a statue. No sound could be heard. They had followed the trail and had gone fifteen miles, while the old dog had cut across the country and headed them off.

He pulled through the mire, clambered over the slippery poles, jumped from root to root and from tuft to tuft, until he gained the opposite side. Here he found a fence that was decayed and tumbling down. It inclosed a field that had been in disuse for several years, and that was overgrown with young pines and dewberry vines. Near the opposite side of the field was an abandoned log cabin. The mud had long ago dropped from the cracks between the logs, the roof was partly gone, the chimney had fallen and was a pile of mud and sticks, the windows had lost their shutters years ago, and the hewn slabs, with which the floor was laid were disarranged and decayed. The berries in the field were ripe, and the dog consumed considerable time in wandering around among the pines, his nose all the while close to the ground and his tail whisking fiercely. The cause is easily explained: the man had picked the berries and breakfasted in the field. The trail was hot, but the dog remained silent, every now and then raising his head and peering about him. The old house was almost hidden by young mulberries and China trees. The dog left the trail finally and trotted to the door of the cabin. He placed his fore feet upon the block that served as a step, and looked cautiously around the interior. His victim lay upon his face in a corner, sound asleep, his forehead resting upon his right arm, and the pistol clasped in his right hand. The dog pricked up his drooping ears and eyed him curiously. He noiselessly gained the doorsill, still keeping his eyes cautiously on the sleeping man. He advanced one foot upon a slab to the right, but it rocked and made a slight noise. He withdrew his foot, and tried another slab on the left. This was steadier, and bore his weight firmly. He put out his foot to try the next slab, but it was unsteady; he tried another, and it rattled. He waited a few moments, and then backed noiselessly through the door and regained the ground.

Another method of approach was left. The wily old dog crept under the sill and proceeded under the house toward the corner in which the deserter slumbered. About three feet from where he lay a slab had been displaced, leaving an opening six feet long and twelve inches wide. The dog cautiously poked his head through the hole, planted his fore paws upon a beam, and gradually brought his shoulders upward until he stood almost erect upon his hind legs. With a dextrous, noiseless spring, he brought his hind feet upon the beam, and stood a moment in this cramped position. Finding the sleeping man still undisturbed, he approached him carefully, taking his steps slowly. He smelled the man's muddy boots, drawing deep and silent inspirations, and sniffed along his entire person until he reached his head, and here he breathed with much greater caution. The man was in his shirt sleeves, and his large, strong neck presented a tempting field for attack. But the dog was old and his fangs were worn with age. He regarded the exposed neck so eagerly, and his whole frame was so rigid, that it seemed he was on the point of taking a desperate step. Had the man lain with his throat uppermost perhaps the dog would not have hesitated. As it was, while he was regarding the bait that tempted him he suddenly pricked up his ears and listened attentively. He heard the yelping of the hounds as they emerged from the canebrake. Stepping cautiously backward he disappeared through the hole, slunk into a dark corner under the cabin, and lay down.

The hounds crossed the fence, noisy, furious, and blood-thirsty. They tore wildly through the patch of berries, and their noise awakened the man. He listened, and then sprang to his feet. In a moment he realized his horrible position—alone, in a vast wilderness, with no human being to assist him in battling with a terrible death, and with a pack of infuriated bloodhounds, trained in the love of human gore, to tear out his heart and strew his entrails upon the earth. His first feeling was one of overpowering terror. He trembled in every joint and his teeth chattered with fear. He looked around wildly and despairingly, and discovered a joist above his head. Securing the pistol in his belt, he sprang upward and caught the joist with his hands. It was old and rotten, and swayed under his weight, but he pulled himself upon it and awaited the dogs.

They rushed blindly into the cabin, foaming and yelp-ing, eagerly smelled the slabs on which the man had slept, ran around the cabin barking and hungry for blood, crawled under the house, scoured the shrubbery, went over the field again, and rushed madly back into the cabin. Knowing that they would find him sooner or later, and that every moment he lost lessened the distance between himself and the human bloodhounds, the man selected the largest and finest looking dog and sent a bullet between his eyes. The hound rolled over with quivering limbs and stiffening muscles. The dogs were thunderstruck, but not dismayed. One strong young hound made a desperate spring and fastened his fangs in the man's heel. He fell with a shot through the brain. The man had three shots left, and he must reserve at least one for a last extremity. He had killed two dogs, and counted nine remaining. With two more well-directed shots he reduced the number to seven.

By this time the fugitive had warmed to his work. The blood tingled in his hands and arms, and he felt his great strength bulging and swelling his muscles. No time was to be lost. He replaced the pistol, stood upon the joist, and pushed a few boards from the roof. Grasping the rotten rafters, he pulled himself upon the roof, and sought a bludgeon. The boards were of oak, and were weighted down with logs, which ran transversely, and which he easily pushed off with his feet. With little difficulty he secured a worm-eaten partially decayed board, four feet long and an inch thick. By striking it over the end of a log he split it, and was thus armed with a powerful weapon. The man was naturally brave, and at this moment his strength seemed so enormous that he felt himself a match for a hundred hounds. The dogs were still in the house, howling and baffled.

Martin crawled carefully to the eaves, and prepared to give battle to the deadly enemy. He looked upon the ground, but the dogs were not visible; and, steadying himself, he dropped heavily and caught nimbly on his feet. He felt that he must finish the fight within half an hour, or he would be confronted with carbines and pistols. The dogs heard him drop, and sprang through the door. The man turned quickly and raised his weapon; the seven dogs made a furious onslaught, but a powerful blow upon the head sent the leader rolling dead upon the ground. The rotten board was strained by the blow, and he must use it more carefully. Six ferocious dogs still confronted him, and two eyes that he did not see blinked at him from under the cabin. The vigor with which the deserter met the attacks, and the threatening attitude that he maintained, disconcerted the dogs, and they ran around him at a safe distance, their teeth glistening, their tails whisking, their heads bent to the ground, the froth dripping from their protruding tongues.

The man suddenly dashed at a dog, and mortally wounded him with a heavy blow on the back of the neck. While he was in the act of striking, and before he could regain his defensive attitude, an active young dog, with fangs as sharp as knives, sprang upon his shoulders and fastened his teeth in the back of the man's neck. The other dogs, emboldened by the success of their companion, made a furious attack from behind. The man faced about, with the fangs of the hound still imbedded in his neck and his back ripped and lacerated with the sharp claws of the suspended dog, and struck about wildly and desperately, breaking the jaw of one and the leg of another. He made one terrible blow, that, in his agony, missed the mark, and his noble bludgeon was shattered against the ground.

The dog gnawed at his neck, and imbedded his fangs still deeper in the flesh, causing the blood to pour down the man's back and breast. At this moment, when the man was paralyzed with pain and frantic at the loss of his weapon, the two dogs still unhurt that confronted him sprang upon him, buried their teeth in his flesh, and bore him to the ground. He sank upon his knees, threw off the two dogs with a mighty effort, and defended his throat with all the desperation and strength that roused his every energy and sustained his failing hopes. They snapped at his hands and tore them, and completely stripped the shirt from his body. They plowed his skin with their claws, and the blood gushed from a hundred wounds. One of the dogs allowed the strong hand of the man to close upon his throat, and then he was flung stunned to the ground. Catching an idea from this maneuver, the man allowed the other hound to seize his arm, then took him by the leg and dashed him against the house.

The deserter was growing faint; but he staggered to his feet, grasped the hind legs of the dog that clung so tenaciously to his neck, snapped the bones as though they were reeds, and jerked him from his hold, tearing the flesh horribly.

By one of those curious eccentricities of fortuitous chance, the man found a weapon in his hands in the dog that he held by the legs, and that snapped at his legs, and writhed and squirmed and howled. The two hounds that he had succeeded in throwing off rallied their strength and returned to the attack cooler and wiser, but none the less terrible. The man backed against the wall, and met the charge by knocking down a dog with the one he held in his hands. Finding that he could not advantageously wield his heavy weapon in such close proximity to the wall, he suddenly advanced and knocked over the other dog in the act. The blows, heavy as they were, did not disable his two antagonists. Every time that he swung down his living bludgeon it became weaker and its struggles more faint. He struck rapidly and carefully, husbanding his strength, yet every now and then missing his object, as it would adroitly evade the blow, and bringing down his heavy club against the ground with a dull thud, crushing its bones and dislocating its vertebrae. In a short while it was but a lifeless mass of broken bones and bruised flesh. The wounded hounds had hidden in the thicket, and the two that remained had become bruised and crippled, and had changed their tactics into harassing their enemy until he had expended all his strength.

The man felt himself growing sick and faint, and he recognized the necessity of immediately bringing the fight to a close by capturing his enemies with strategy. He threw aside his weapon, but the dogs simply glared at him. If he could only get them in his clutches again he would be saved, but experience had made them cunning. So he suddenly threw up his hands and fell, and they sprang for his throat. Quick as a cat he seized a throat in each hand, turned them over upon the ground with great difficulty, planted his great knees upon their breasts, and, crushing their ribs with his remaining strength, choked them until their eyes almost burst from their sockets, until their tongues swelled and hung from their mouths, and until life was extinct.

The terrible fight had lasted two hours. The man staggered to his feet and looked around. Not a soul was in sight. He drew a deep breath, and his naked, bloody chest swelled with triumph. But the loss of blood and the extreme pain of his wounds had so exhausted him that he felt the ground rising to strike him in the face, and, with a heavy lunge, he lay extended upon the ground.

Two glittering eyes, followed by the neck and shoulders of a hound, emerged from under the cabin. The Tiger crept forward softly, but darted back as the man with a desperate effort rose to his hands and knees. The deserter battled bravely with unconsciousness, but was dying of thirst. He crawled painfully along a disused path leading to a spring, while the blood streamed upon the ground. On reaching the spring, he drank greedily, and bathed his face and head. The blood poured from his wounds and changed to the color of wine the little stream that flowed from the spring. The dog had followed him unseen, and was crouching behind a thick clump of shrubbery. The man, refreshed by the water, again staggered to his feet, but the pines swam before his eyes and he fell unconscious to the ground. The old dog approached cautiously, and, when within a few feet of his prey, sprang forward and closed his powerful jaws upon the throat of the fainting man.

A woman, pale and haggard, and with the wild light of insanity in her eyes, sat on the ground and held the head of her husband in her lap, and rocked and moaned, and sang, and cried, and called him vainly. The eyes that stared at the sky were so terribly bloodshot, and the face was so black, and the features so distorted, that it is strange she recognized as her husband the disfigured, lifeless body of Martin, the deserter.

Affair at St. Albans

Herbert Ravenel Sass

There were three hotels in the little town of St. Albans, Vermont, fifteen miles from the Canadian border, and one day in the fall of '64 a young man who had just got off the train from Montreal stopped at the station ticket window to ask about them.

"Why, we're right proud o' them," Dodson, the station agent, told him. "They're nice places for a town of five thousand, and when the new Welden House is finished, it'll be a beauty."

Dodson sized the man up as either an angler or some sort of traveling salesman because of the kind of valise he carried—a leather bag slung by a strap from his right shoulder. Except for this unusual valise, which reminded the ticket agent vaguely of something that he couldn't quite fix in his mind, there was nothing remarkable about the stranger.

From the depot he strolled up Lake Street, keeping his overcoat buttoned, though it was a rather warm morning for October. As he reached the St. Albans House, the first of the three hotels, he seemed to slow his pace a little, but he didn't stop there and, going on up the slope toward Main Street, his steps quickened. At the corner of Lake and Main, a second hotel, the American House, stood where it is today, and again the young man seemed to walk more slowly as he passed it. One might almost have thought that he expected something to happen, but nothing did. Turning the corner, he walked north up Main Street, where a good many people were moving. When he got to the third hotel, the Tremont House—where the city hall now stands—his steps again lagged just a little.

But this time the slackening of his pace was only momentary. Somebody in an upper-front room of the Tremont, a window of which was open, was whistling The Battle Cry of Freedom:

> *The Union forever, hurrah, boys, hurrah!*
> *Down with the traitor; up with the Star!*
> *While we rally round the Flag, boys,*
>   *Rally once again,*
> *Shouting the battle cry of Freedom!*

The lips of the young man down in the street moved in time with the whistling as though framing the words of the song: everybody knew that rousing lyric of the Chicago music teacher, George Root, and in that passionate autumn of '64, when Sherman had taken Atlanta and Sheridan was sweeping through the Shenandoah Valley, thousands north of Mason and Dixon's Line were whistling it. The young man in the overcoat, now stepping briskly along, walked nearly to the corner of Kingman Street, where the Bank of St. Albans stood, and under his broad-brimmed hat his black eyes studied the bank. E.D. Fuller, the livery-stable owner, happened by just then, and the stranger asked him whether there were any other hotels farther up Main Street where he might engage a room—an odd question to ask because Dodson had already told him there were only three hotels. Upon being answered in the negative, he thanked Fuller courteously, retraced his steps to the Tremont House and went in.

At the desk, however, he didn't engage a room. He introduced himself as Thomas B. Collins, of Montreal, and asked for Mr. Bennett Young, of the same city. "Mr. Young," he told the clerk with easy affability, "was to have arrived here yesterday. I hope he hasn't been delayed."

Skinner, the clerk, reassured him, "Mr. Young's here, sir. A most agreeable gentleman. Room Twenty-three, third door on the left from the head of the stairs."

On the second floor, the wooden partitions were thin. As he walked along the passage, he could hear the man in Room 23 no longer whistling The Battle Cry of Freedom, but humming it. The stranger tapped on the door and, a moment later, entered. After about two hours, he came downstairs, nodded pleasantly to the clerk and went out into the street, again wearing his overcoat, his valise hanging by its strap from his shoulder. That was a curious-looking valise, Skinner said to himself. It reminded the clerk of something—he couldn't say exactly what.

All this would hardly be considered important in itself. But next morning, upon the arrival of the train from Montreal, two more strangers got off—two men in overcoats with an odd bulge over their left hips—and walked from the depot up Lake Street, slowing their pace perceptibly as they passed the St. Albans House, as though they expected something to happen there. In this they were disappointed, but as they turned from Lake Street into Main in front of the American House, somebody in an upper room of that hotel was whistling The Battle Cry of Freedom.

The two men didn't stop at once. They walked on up North Main Street, crossed to the other side and turned south, strolled for a while on the village green, then came back to the American House and inquired at the desk for Mr. Thomas B. Collins, of Montreal. "Room Twenty-seven," the clerk directed them. "Seventh door on the left from the top of the stairs."

An hour later, the pair came down and one of them registered, signing his name as Alamanda P. Bruce, of Toronto, and announcing that he was going to share Mr. Collins' room. The other, a pleasant, talkative fellow, introduced himself as Turner Teavis, of St. John. He and his friends, he said in the course of a ten minutes' chat, were members of a Canadian sportsmen's club assembling in St. Albans for a fishing trip on Lake Champlain. He didn't register and, as he turned away from the desk and walked to the street door, the clerk noticed that his overcoat hung crooked because of an odd-looking bulge on the left side.

None of this would have been of great importance either, except that on the train from Montreal the following morning another pair of strangers arrived in St. Albans, and these had no bulges under their overcoats because they wore their odd-looking strap valises outside, as Thomas Collins had worn his. Again those valises reminded the ticket agent vaguely of something he'd seen somewhere, and he scratched his head trying to hit upon what it was. The two walked off up Lake Street, and this time it happened at the first hotel they came to, the St. Albans House—somebody in an upper-front room was whistling The Battle Cry of Freedom.

The man who was whistling this time showed himself at the window; he was the same man who, the day before, had gone to the American House with Alamanda P. Bruce and later on had left that hostelry. The newcomers glanced up at him, but didn't stop. They walked on up Lake Street to the village green, and fully an hour passed before they entered the St. Albans House and inquired at the desk for Mr. Turner Teavis, of St. John. "Room Twenty-four," the clerk told them. "Fourth door to the right from the top of the stairs."

By Wednesday, October nineteenth, Lt. Bennett Young, of the Confederate Army, with headquarters in Room 23 of the Tremont House, St. Albans, Vermont, had most of his worries behind him. The matter of the haversacks, for instance. Some legalistic adviser of the Confederate commissioners in Canada had declared these kit bags necessary to the expedition because, as a regular part of Confederate field equipment, they would help to establish the legitimacy of the invading force. But it turned out that when the bags were worn under the overcoats, they made an unseemly bulge. Therefore some of the men, coming down from Montreal singly or in pairs, had arrived in St. Albans wearing the haversacks boldly outside their coats. That was risky—just as registering at the St. Albans hotels under their own names was risky, though necessary—and it had worried Lieutenant Young. Even if nobody in St. Albans had ever seen a Confederate soldier in field equipment, they'd all seen pictures in the illustrated magazines, sketched by special artists at the front.

But by October nineteenth, when he had been in St. Albans nearly ten days, Bennett Young had stopped worrying about the haversacks. He wasn't given to worrying about anything overlong. That was one reason why, at the age of twenty-one, he had been chosen to command the Confederate Army in Vermont, the most advanced of all the land forces of the Confederacy.

That was no job for a worrying man. Stretched on his bed in the Tremont House, waiting for Tom Collins, he said to himself that it wasn't a job for any cavalryman. Not for a bluegrass Kentuckian from Jessamine County who'd ridden with John Morgan until Morgan's troopers took a notion they could raid into Ohio in face of 50,000 bluecoats, and most of them had got captured for their brashness. He had escaped from Camp Douglas, outside Chicago, and had slipped across the line into Canada. And now here he was in charge of a Confederate army of twenty men—escaped prisoners like himself, and adept by now at concealing any Southern tricks of speech they may have had—invading the most rock-ribbed Yankee state in the whole of Mr. Lincoln's Union.

Well, it was good strategy and a lot might come of it. When the shooting started and the telegraph wires began to hum and headlines in the papers shouted that the United States was being invaded from the north, there'd be something like panic. Lincoln might have to draw troops from the battle fronts to steady nerves from Maine to Michigan, and that would relieve the pressure on Lee in Virginia. Besides, it was time to do a little retaliating for Sherman's looting in Georgia and Sheridan's burning in the Shenandoah. But all the same, it hadn't been, so far, a cavalryman's job, and Bennett Young was almost sorry that Tom Collins hadn't been put in charge of it.

He was tired of Room 23 at the Tremont House; tired of spying through a peephole on the little priest in the next room whom at first he had suspected of being a spy; tired of tramping on his two legs about the streets of St. Albans pretending to be a Canadian sportsman, getting ready for a fishing trip on Lake Champlain, when actually he was studying this pretty Yankee town and getting ready to kick it in the pants. He was about ready now, thank heaven. Tomorrow the fun would begin, and tomorrow he hoped to feel a good nag under him again. He had his horse picked out—that blaze-faced sorrel mare that E.D. Fuller, the livery-stable owner, used as his personal mount. Tom Collins had his eye on that little beauty too. When the time came, he'd have to beat Tom to her.

There was a tap on the door and, before Young could move, Collins came in. One glance at his face jerked Young upright on the bed. "Lord, Tom!" he exclaimed. "What's happened?"

Collins bent till his dark face was close to Young's. "That priest," he whispered, jerking his head toward the partition. "He was right ahead of me coming upstairs, and he was about to tell me something, but some other people came along. At his door he held his hand up to his eye like this."

Collins cupped his hand in front of his right eye and squinted through it as though looking through a telescope. He dropped his hand and stood staring at Young, his thin face with its line of black mustache twisted in bitter disappointment. "We're whipped before we start, Bennett. There wasn't any doubt about what he meant. He knows about the peephole we cut in the partition. When he put his hand up like that and looked through it, he was telling me that he knows. Bennett, it's what we figured when we started watching him. That priest in there is a Union spy and smart as hell. He's been watching us through our own peephole. Our game's up."

Bennett Young had a moment of black whirling terror such as he used to have every time he saw a line of bluecoats stiffen to meet a charge of Morgan's men. That terror would grip him for a few awful seconds, then it would pass, and when it was over, he'd still be riding in the right direction, not far behind Morgan or Bob Martin or whoever happened to be in command. The terror ended now almost before it had begun and, sitting on the edge of the bed, looking up at Tom Collins, he saw in a flash that there was something wrong about this, something that didn't fit. If this priest in the next room was a Yankee spy after all, why had he practically told Collins so; why had he given himself away?

He got up and, taking his pocketknife from the table, tiptoed in his stocking feet to the partition. Lifting the flap of wallpaper, he used the thin blade of the knife to remove the wooden peg with which he had plugged the peephole. He waited a minute, then another minute; it wouldn't be nice to have a bullet come through that peephole into his eye. When at length he applied his eye to the aperture, he saw that the priest had retired behind a screen near the bed; he could see the man's black robe lying on the floor by the screen. He watched quietly, waiting for the priest to reappear. Instead of the priest, a woman stepped from behind the screen.

Bennett Young watched, astounded. She was young, not pretty at first glance, very slim-waisted, her hair dusky rather than black, drawn close and caught in a knot behind. It must have been drawn even closer, Young realized, when, in her priest's role, it had been covered by a wig. The dress which she had just put on behind the screen was of light gray stuff, a little crinkled from having been folded tightly, and there was no petticoat under it, for, as she stooped to pick up the priest's robe, he could see the outline of her thighs. She moved with swift sureness. Her deft fingers stuffed the robe into a bag which she carried; then they twisted a gray scarf around her head, transforming it into a turban or toque. This done, she walked straight toward the peephole, and Bennett Young, too dumfounded to be afraid, said to himself again that still she wasn't exactly pretty and yet the turban had done something for her.

She stood close to the peephole, her slightly aquiline profile on a level with it. "You're all so young," she said, her voice a little husky—a completely feminine voice, yet one that could easily imitate a man's. "You're just a parcel of boys. Why, there isn't one of you except the one named Joe—Joe McGorty, isn't it?—who's even as old as I am. I think that's why Mr. Clay (with enormous relief Bennett Young realized that she meant former Senator Clay, of Alabama, one of the Confederate commissioners in Canada) sent me on here ahead of you to look things over and maybe help you."

She could talk to him as though he were a child—she couldn't be more than twenty-four herself—and not offend him; that in itself, he realized vaguely, was something to wonder at. He started to speak, but she stopped him. "There isn't time, lieutenant. I'm clever at this kind of work—I've been a secret agent three years—and I can tell you things are stirring. The town's beginning to wonder about the Canadian sportsmen's club. You can't wait any longer. It'll have to be today; you'll have to start your Battle of St. Albans today."

She paused, but before he could say anything, she went on briskly. "That's what I wanted to tell you; it's today or never. And I'm moving out now. I think there'll be two detectives—I could even tell you their names—at the depot this afternoon, looking for a priest, and I wouldn't want them to find out that sometimes the priest turns into a woman. So I'm just fading away, lieutenant. I'm going back to Mr. Clay across the line, and I'm not going by train. There's a footpath across the hills and along Missisquoi Bay that's only fourteen miles to the Canada border. I'll be there before dark, and I wish I could take you along."

He heard a low laugh. "You can't get a word in edgeways, can you, lieutenant? You see, I don't get many chances to converse on these trips, and when I do—" Leaving her sentence unfinished, she turned and looked straight at the peephole. "I'm a little superstitious about good-bys," she said lightly. "We'll just make a song of this one." With mock solemnity, she sang the opening phrases of Just Before the Battle, Mother. It was completely silly—and completely charming. In another moment she was through the doorway and out in the passage. Bennett Young ran to the door of his own room and jerked it open. He was in time to see the top of her turban for an instant as she went down the stairs.

"The reporter who substitutes romance for facts runs a risk," Hocking, of Harvard, used to tell his students, "but the reporter who offers facts without their inherent romance is surely lying." There is little in the record about the woman in Room 21. But—to anticipate—five weeks after this, on November twenty-fifth, Bennett Young wrote in high spirits from Canada to the clerk of the Tremont House, enclosing a check—on the Bank of St. Albans!—in payment for his room. In this letter he remarked that he had left there, among other articles, a flask of Old Rifle whiskey, and in it, too, he recalled with pleasure "the young lady who occupied the room adjoining mine" and whose "siren voice" singing Just Before the Battle, Mother "gave me great encouragement for the work before us." Of the dozens of songs that she might have chosen, why did she choose that one, unless she knew what was about to happen? And how could she know what was about to happen, unless she was a Southern secret agent in touch with the whole plan? Moreover, still later, when Bennett Young was on trial in Canada and his life was in peril, a woman secret agent of the Confederacy, who, it seems, sometimes dressed as a priest—But that came afterward and had best be told at the proper time.

They took, it is reasonable to suppose, a warming dram of Old Rifle; Tom Collins swore happily that the stuff would kill at 40 yards. Before Collins left, Bennett Young got his gray uniform out of his haversack and put it on. It must have been Collins who spread the word quietly to certain rooms in the three hotels and to certain private dwellings which had recently taken lodgers. There was no hitch. As the town clock struck three, twenty men who had been strolling in scattered yet related groups along Main Street threw off their overcoats to reveal Confederate uniforms, each man with a pair of navy six-shooters in his belt. They moved with the sureness of veterans, and Bennett Young had time for a flash of pride as he swept his eye up and down Main Street and saw his Kentuckians—nearly all the twenty were Kentuckians—going smoothly into action.

"In the name of the Confederate States," he shouted, "I take possession of St. Albans!"

Many people were in the street, townfolk and farmers from the surrounding country. They stood open-mouthed and staring, shocked beyond speech or action by the gray uniforms. This apparition which they saw before them—it was a dream, a nightmare, wholly impossible. The war was something a thousand miles away, to be read about in newspapers; it couldn't come to St. Albans. Bennett Young strode through a throng that shrank before the tall figure in rebel gray as though it were a lion on the loose. Actually, he felt embarrassingly helpless. He couldn't fight on foot, damn it—no man from Jessamine County could. He'd told Alamanda Bruce to stick close to him, acting as his aide, and now, with Bruce behind him, pistols drawn, he stalked into Fuller's livery stable.

The sorrel mare had the second stall. He got her out while Alamanda Bruce held off Fuller's astounded hostlers. Saddle and bridle were on their pegs. In two minutes Young had them on the mare, and then he was on her back.

"Bring out your horses," he ordered the older hostler, "all of them. Get saddles on them and bring them outside....See to it, Bruce."

He wheeled the mare out through the wide doorway of the stable and looked southward down Main Street. The shock of surprise still held; the people on the sidewalks milled about or stood in gaping groups. Beyond the American House a farmer, standing up in his wagon, was lashing his team in headlong flight.

Young galloped down Main, high in his stirrups, people scattering before him. As far as he could tell, things were going according to plan. Three squads had been detailed to raid the three St. Albans banks, seizing all enemy funds and securities for the Richmond government. Another squad was herding citizens onto the village green. A third was commandeering horses. A fourth group would break bottles of liquid Greek fire against certain buildings. Near Young, McGorty and another Confederate stopped a farmer's wagon opposite the Franklin County Bank. They loosed the trace chains of the two big Shires, stripped off their harness and mounted bareback, using the headstalls as bridles.

Except for Young's voice giving an occasional order, all had been strangely silent so far; men's tongues as well as their limbs seemed paralyzed. Now, abruptly, a shot smashed this eerie stillness. A man dashed out of Fields' livery stable, stopped suddenly, snatched his hat from his head and stood in amazement, staring at a hole in its crown.

From Fields' stable, three frightened horses, evidently saddled before the shot startled them, came plunging. One jerked loose and ran away up the street, but Young saw Dan Butterworth and Caleb Wallace bring the two others under control and mount. That was first rate; he was getting his men on horseback fast. What about Fuller's, where he had left Alamanda Bruce?

He rode there just as six saddled horses were led out by Bruce and the two hostlers. He didn't see E.D. Fuller behind a tree in front of Dutcher's drugstore, aiming a revolver at him. Three times Fuller pulled the trigger, and each time the pistol snapped. Young turned and saw him. He'd chatted and talked horses with the big liveryman, and liked him.

"Now, now, Mr. Fuller," he chided. "How about running into Bedard's store yonder and getting me a pair of spurs?"

Fuller ran into Bedard's, passed through the shop and through the back lot to the unfinished Welden House, where Elinas J. Morrison, a Manchester contractor, had a gang working. It took him a while to make himself understood— Morrison thought him drunk or crazy. At last Morrison realized that the incredible was happening. He called his men down from their work on the building, and as they started for Main Street they heard a pistol shot, then two more in quick succession.

Young and Bruce, leading their six horses, had met the first of the bank-raiding squads—Tom Collins and three others. Collins was talkative, as he always was in action; he'd told Young once that he had to talk and laugh at such times or else he'd cry.

"By Jove, Bennett," he said, "you should have seen us in the St. Albans Bank. We cleaned 'em. If it takes a thousand dollars to pay for each Yankee soldier, we've got a hundred prisoners in these haversacks." He swung himself up on a horse, the three men with him did likewise, and they galloped on.

Near the corner of Lake Street, opposite the village green, Young saw three men in gray dash out of the Franklin County Bank, and almost at the same moment three more emerged from the National Bank, the last man walking backward, both pistols raised. He could see that their kit bags bulged, and somehow he didn't like it. This was enemy money, and now it would go to help the Confederacy; nevertheless, even in war, bank looting seemed a shade off color. Two Confederates—he saw that they were Charles Swager and Dudley Moore—rode around the corner of the American House, leading four saddled horses. Evidently they had come from Gillmore's stable, on Lake Street. These, with the horses taken from Fuller's and Fields' stables and from farmers' wagons, ought to be enough.

"Get 'em up, Bruce!" He pointed with his pistol to the two bank-raiding squads that were still on foot. "Get 'em mounted! Get 'em mounted!"

At his elbow, Turner Teavis pointed at the American House. Smoke was rising from the hotel's windows and from the Atwood store next to it. "Maybe that Greek fire's some good, after all," Teavis drawled.

There was the crack of a rifle, a puff of smoke at a second-story window. Teavis and Young both fired at the smoke, wood splintered, glass crashed to the street.

Almost at once came another shot from a window, then two more. Behind Young, several gray horsemen were replying to this fire. Across Main Street, a man—it was Henry

Watson, a tailor—groaned, clutched his stomach and slumped back against Twiggs' shop. Beyond the width of the street, the crowd of townfolk, herded together on the village green and guarded by two Confederates, was melting away as men at the rear of it broke and ran. Evidently some of them were getting up into the buildings along the street and finding weapons. Suddenly from a half-dozen windows along Main Street burst puffs of smoke lit with flame.

In the St. Albans telegraph office an excited operator was tapping out a message to Gov. John Gregory Smith at the state capital, Montpelier. "Southern raiders are in St. Albans," the message said, "shooting citizens, burning houses." This done, the operator left his instrument, carefully locked his office door and ran toward the sound of the shooting. That afternoon Secretary of War Stanton in Washington received word that a great battle was raging at Cedar Creek, Virginia, which imperiled the capital. A few minutes later came the astounding news that the United States was being invaded by a Confederate army from Canada which had already captured St. Albans, Vermont.

Capt. George Conger, of the 1st Vermont Cavalry, just back from the front in Virginia, drove into St. Albans that October afternoon, to be halted by a man in Confederate gray near the American House. Though a navy six-shooter backed up the order to surrender, Conger dashed down Lake Street and got away unscathed. Men from the railroad shops and some who had escaped from the village green were gathering with what weapons they could snatch up.

Captain Conger led them up Lake Street toward Main, where the gray riders were shooting it out with townsmen firing from the upper windows.

"Time to go, lieutenant!" Tom Collins sang out happily. "Here come Ethan Allen and his Green Mountain Boys! Time for old Kentucky to pull her freight!"

High time! Vermont, granite-jawed and madder than any hornet, was getting into action. Bennett Young formed his horsemen in columns of fours. With Young and Collins acting as rear guard, the Confederates retreated up Main Street. Near the giant elm that still stands opposite the city hall, Elinas Morrison was mortally hit, another townsman wounded.

160

To the north end of town the slow retreat continued; after that, details are lost in a thunder of hoofs and a cloud of dust. Some say that halfway to the Canadian line the Confederates set fire to a hay wagon on the covered bridge over Black Creek, burned the bridge and thumbed their noses at the baffled pursuers. Others declare that the fire was put out promptly and the bridge saved. In any case, Bennett Young brought his whole force safely across the Canadian border with more than $200,000 of United States money in his haversacks for the hard-pressed Confederate treasury at Richmond, leaving behind him such an excitement on the telegraph wires and such an uproar in the northern tier of states as hadn't been known since Bull Run.

What, beyond that, was accomplished is a question. This northernmost land engagement of the Civil War did not force Mr. Lincoln to pull back troops from the front; the pressure on Lee was not diminished. Damage to St. Albans was slight. Though the Canadian Government, which had arrested fourteen of the raiders, refused the first Federal demand for extradition and released the Southerners, Lieutenant Young and five of his men were rearrested and brought to trial in Montreal, while Canada reimbursed the St. Albans banks to the extent of $50,000—the rest being permanently lost.

For Bennett Young the outlook was dark. His life hung on the question of whether a messenger could get through the Union lines to Richmond and bring back official papers establishing his status as commander of an authorized Confederate force. Several volunteers failed, but two succeeded, returning to Montreal with duplicate copies on the same day. One was a chaplain, the Rev. S.F. Cameron, of Maryland. The other was a young woman, a secret agent of the Confederacy, a widow of twenty-four whose name has been lost, though her photograph, given to one of the St. Albans Confederates, survives. An oval, slightly aquiline face, quick with intelligence; fine eyebrows, a straight, firm mouth and cleanly chiseled chin; dark hair drawn close and caught in a knot behind. One likes to think that it was her copy of the papers, not the good chaplain's, which, just as the trial was about to end, saved Bennett Young's life.

The Second Missouri Compromise

OWEN WISTER

I

The Legislature had sat up all night, much absorbed, having taken off its coat because of the stove. This was the fortieth and final day of its first session under an order of things not new only, but novel. It sat with the retrospect of forty days' duty done, and the prospect of forty days' consequent pay to come. Sleepy it was not, but wide and wider awake over a progressing crisis. Hungry it had been until after a breakfast fetched to it from the Overland at seven, three hours ago. It had taken no intermission to wash its face, nor was there just now any apparatus for this, as the tin pitcher commonly used stood not in the basin in the corner, but on the floor by the Governor's chair; so the eyes of the Legislature, though earnest, were dilapidated. Last night the pressure of public business had seemed over, and no turning back the hands of the clock likely to be necessary. Besides Governor Ballard, Mr. Hewley, Secretary and Treasurer, was sitting up too, small, iron-gray, in feature and bearing every inch the capable, dignified official, but his necktie had slipped off during the night. The bearded Councillors had the best of it, seeming after their vigil less stale in the face than the member from Silver City, for instance, whose day-old black growth blurred his dingy chin, or the member from Big Camas, whose scantier red crop bristled on his cheeks in sparse wandering arrangements, like spikes on the barrel of a musical box. For comfort, most of the pistols were on the table with the Statutes of the United States. Secretary and Treasurer Hewley's lay on his strong-box immediately behind him. The Governor's was a light one, and always hung in the armhole of his waistcoat. The graveyard of Boisé City this year had twenty-seven tenants, two brought there by meningitis, and twenty-five by difference of opinion. Many denizens of the Territory were miners, and the unsettling element of gold-dust hung in the air, breeding argument. The early, thin, bright morning steadily mellowed against the windows distant from the stove; the panes melted clear until they ran, steamed faintly, and dried, this fresh May day, after the night's untimely cold; while still the Legislature sat in its shirt-sleeves, and several statesmen had removed their boots. Even had appearances counted, the session was invisible from the street. Unlike a good number of houses in the town, the State-House (as they called it from old habit) was not all on the ground-floor for outsiders to stare into, but up a flight of wood steps to a wood gallery. From this, to be sure, the interior could be watched from several windows on both sides; but the journey up the steps was precisely enough to disincline the idle, and this was counted a sensible thing by the lawmakers. They took the ground that shaping any government for a raw wilderness community needed seclusion, and they set a high value upon unworried privacy.

The sun had set upon a concentrated Council, but it rose upon faces that looked momentous. Only the Governor's and Treasurer's were impassive, and they concealed something even graver than the matter in hand.

"I'll take a hun'red mo', Gove'nuh," said the member from Silver City, softly, his eyes on space. His name was Powhattan Wingo.

The Governor counted out the blue, white, and red chips to Wingo, pencilled some figures on a thickly ciphered and cancelled paper that bore in print the words "Territory of Idaho, Council Chamber," and then filled up his glass from the tin pitcher, adding a little sugar.

"And I'll trouble you fo' the toddy," Wingo added, always softly, and his eyes always on space. "Raise you ten, suh." This was to the Treasurer. Only the two were playing at present. The Governor was kindly acting as bank; the others were looking on.

"And ten," said the Treasurer.

"And ten," said Wingo.

"And twenty," said the Treasurer.

"And fifty," said Wingo, gently bestowing his chips in the middle of the table.

The Treasurer called.

The member from Silver City showed down five high hearts, and a light rustle went over the Legislature when the Treasurer displayed three twos and a pair of threes, and gathered in his harvest. He had drawn two cards, Wingo one; and losing to the lowest hand that could have beaten you is under such circumstances truly hard luck. Moreover, it was almost the only sort of luck that had attended Wingo since about half after three that morning. Seven hours of cards just a little lower than your neighbor's is searching to the nerves.

"Gove'nuh, I'll take a hun'red mo'," said Wingo; and once again the Legislature rustled lightly, and the new deal began.

Treasurer Hewley's winnings flanked his right, a pillared fortress on the table, built chiefly of Wingo's misfortunes. Hewley had not counted them, and his architecture was for neatness and not ostentation; yet the Legislature watched him arrange his gains with sullen eyes. It would have pleased him now to lose; it would have more than pleased him to be able to go to bed quite a long time ago. But winners cannot easily go to bed. The thoughtful Treasurer bet his money and deplored this luck. It seemed likely to trap himself and the Governor in a predicament they had not foreseen. All had taken a hand at first, and played for several hours, until Fortune's wheel ran into a rut deeper than usual. Wingo slowly became the loser to several, then Hewley had forged ahead, winner from everybody. One by one they had dropped out, each meaning to go home, and all lingering to see the luck turn. It was an extraordinary run, a rare specimen, a breaker of records, something to refer to in the future as a standard of measure and an embellishment of reminiscence; quite enough to keep the Idaho Legislature up all night. And then it was their friend who was losing. The only speaking in the room was the brief card talk of the two players.

"Five better," said Hewley, winner again four times in the last five.

"Ten," said Wingo.

"And twenty," said the Secretary and Treasurer.

"Call you."

"Three kings."

"They are good, suh. Gove'nuh, I'll take a hun'red mo'."

Upon this the wealthy and weary Treasurer made a try for liberty and bed. How would it do, he suggested, to have a round of jack-pots, say ten—or twenty, if the member from Silver City preferred—and then stop? It would do excellently, the member said, so softly that the Governor looked at him. But Wingo's large countenance remained inexpressive, his black eyes still impersonally fixed on space. He sat thus till his chips were counted to him, and then the eyes moved to watch the cards fall. The Governor hoped he might win now, under the jack-pot system. At noon he should have a disclosure to make; something that would need the most cheerful and contented feelings in Wingo and the Legislature to be received with any sort of calm. Wingo was behind the game to the tune of—the Governor gave up adding as he ran his eye over the figures of the bank's erased and tormented record, and he shook his head to himself. This was inadvertent.

"May I inquah who yo're shakin' yoh head at, suh?" said Wingo, wheeling upon the surprised Governor.

"Certainly," answered that official. "You." He was never surprised for very long. In 1867 it did not do to remain surprised in Idaho.

"And have I done anything which meets yoh disapprobation?" pursued the member from Silver City, enunciating with care.

"You have met my disapprobation."

Wingo's eye was on the Governor, and now his friends drew a little together, and as a unit sent a glance of suspicion at the lone bank.

"You will gratify me by being explicit, suh," said Wingo to the bank.

"Well, you've emptied the toddy."

"Ha-ha, Gove'nuh! I rose, suh, to yoh little fly. We'll awduh some mo'."

"Time enough when he comes for the breakfast things," said Governor Ballard, easily.

"As you say, suh. I'll open for five dolluhs." Wingo turned back to his game. He was winning, and as his luck continued his voice ceased to be soft, and became a shade truculent. The Governor's ears caught this change, and he also noted the lurking triumph in the faces of Wingo's fellow-statesmen. Cheerfulness and content were scarcely reigning yet in the Council Chamber of Idaho as Ballard sat watching the friendly game. He was beginning to fear that he must leave the Treasurer alone and take some precautions outside. But he would have to be separated for some time from his ally, cut off from giving him any hints. Once the Treasurer looked at him, and he immediately winked reassuringly, but the Treasurer failed to respond. Hewley might be able to wink after everything was over, but he could not find it in his serious heart to do so now. He was wondering what would happen if this game should last till noon with the company in its present mood. Noon was the time fixed for paying the Legislative Assembly the compensation due for its services during this session; and the Governor and the Treasurer had put their heads together and arranged a surprise for the Legislative Assembly. They were not going to pay them.

A knock sounded at the door, and on seeing the waiter from the Overland enter, the Governor was seized with an idea. Perhaps precaution could be taken from the inside. "Take this pitcher," said he, "and have it refilled with the same. Joseph knows my mixture." But Joseph was night bar-tender, and now long in his happy bed, with a day successor in the saloon, and this one did not know the mixture. Ballard had foreseen this when he spoke, and that his writing a note of directions would seem quite natural.

"The receipt is as long as the drink," said a legislator, watching the Governor's pencil fly.

"He don't know where my private stock is located," explained Ballard. The waiter departed with the breakfast things and the note, and while the jack-pots continued the Governor's mind went carefully over the situation.

Until lately the Western citizen has known one every-day experience that no dweller in our thirteen original colonies has had for two hundred years. In Massachusetts they have not seen it since 1641; in Virginia not since 1628. It is that of belonging to a community of which every adult was born somewhere else. When you come to think of this a little it is dislocating to many of your conventions. Let a citizen of Salem, for instance, or a well-established Philadelphia Quaker, try to imagine his chief-justice fresh from Louisiana, his mayor from Arkansas, his tax-collector from South Carolina, and himself recently arrived in a wagon from a thousand-mile drive. To be governor of such a community Ballard had travelled in a wagon from one quarter of the horizon; from another quarter Wingo had arrived on a mule. People reached Boisé in three ways: by rail to a little west of the Missouri, after which it was wagon, saddle, or walk for the remaining fifteen hundred miles; from California it was shorter; and from Portland, Oregon, only about five hundred miles, and some of these more agreeable, by water up the Columbia. Thus it happened that salt often sold for its weight in gold-dust. A miner in the Bannock Basin would meet a freight teamster coming in with the staples of life, having journeyed perhaps sixty consecutive days through the desert, and valuing his salt highly. The two accordingly bartered in scales, white powder against yellow, and both parties content. Some in Boisé to-day can remember these bargains. After all, they were struck but thirty years ago. Governor Ballard and Treasurer Hewley did not come from the same place, but they constituted a minority of two in Territorial politics because they hailed from north of Mason and Dixon's line. Powhattan Wingo and the rest of the Council were from Pike County, Missouri. They had been Secessionists, some of them Knights of the Golden Circle; they had belonged to Price's Left Wing, and they flocked together. They were seven—two lying unwell at the Overland, five now present in the State-House with the Governor and Treasurer. Wingo, Gascon Claiborne, Gratiot des Pères, Pete Cawthon, and F. Jackson Gilet were their names. Besides this Council of seven were thirteen members of the Idaho House of Representatives, mostly of the same political feather with the Council, and they too would be present at noon to receive their pay. How Ballard and Hewley came to be a minority of two is a simple matter. Only twenty-five months had gone since Appomattox Court-House. That surrender was presently followed by Johnston's to Sherman, at Durhams Station, and following this the various Confederate armies in Alabama, or across the Mississippi, or wherever they happened to be, had successively surrendered—but not Price's Left Wing. There was the wide open West under its nose, and no Grant or Sherman infesting that void. Why surrender? Wingos, Claibornes, and all, they melted away. Price's Left Wing sailed into the prairie and passed below the horizon. To know what it next did you must, like Ballard or Hewley, pass below the horizon yourself, clean out of sight of the dome at Washington to remote, untracked Idaho. There, besides wild red men in quantities, would you find not very tame white ones, gentlemen of the ripest Southwestern persuasion, and a Legislature to fit. And if, like Ballard or Hewley, you were a Union man, and the President of the United States had appointed you Governor or Secretary of such a place, your days would be full of awkwardness, though your difference in creed might not hinder you from playing draw-poker with the unreconstructed. These Missourians were whole-souled, ample-natured males in many ways, but born with a habit of hasty shooting. The Governor, on setting foot in Idaho, had begun to study pistolship, but acquired thus in middle life it could never be with him that spontaneous art which it was with Price's Left Wing. Not that the weapons now lying loose about the State-House were brought for use there. Everybody always went armed in Boisé, as the gravestones impliedly testified. Still, the thought of the bad quarter of an hour which it might come to at noon did cross Ballard's mind, raising the image of a column in the morrow's paper: "An unfortunate occurrence has ended relations between esteemed gentlemen hitherto the warmest personal friends.... They will be laid to rest at 3 P.M.... As a last token of respect for our lamented Governor, the troops from Boisé Barracks...." The Governor trusted that if his friends at the post were to do him any service it would not be a funeral one.

The new pitcher of toddy came from the Overland, the jack-pots continued, were nearing a finish, and Ballard began to wonder if anything had befallen a part of his note to the bar-tender, an enclosure addressed to another person.

"Ha, suh!" said Wingo to Hewley. "My pot again, I declah." The chips had been crossing the table his way, and he was now loser but six hundred dollars.

"Ye ain't goin' to whip Mizzooruh all night an' all day, ez a rule," observed Pete Cawthon, Councillor from Lost Leg.

"'Tis a long road that has no turnin', Gove'nuh," said F. Jackson Gilet, more urbanely. He had been in public life in Missouri, and was now President of the Council in Idaho. He, too, had arrived on a mule, but could at will summon a rhetoric dating from Cicero, and preserved by many luxuriant orators until after the middle of the present century.

"True," said the Governor, politely. "But here sits the long suffering bank, whichever way the road turns. I'm sleepy."

"You sacrifice yo'self in the good cause," replied Gilet, pointing to the poker game. "Oneasy lies the head that wahs an office, suh." And Gilet bowed over his compliment.

The Governor thought so indeed. He looked at the Treasurer's strong-box, where lay the appropriation lately made by Congress to pay the Idaho Legislature for its services; and he looked at the Treasurer, in whose pocket lay the key of the strong-box. He was accountable to the Treasury at Washington for all money disbursed for Territorial expenses.

"Eleven twenty," said Wingo, "and only two hands mo' to play."

The Governor slid out his own watch.

"I'll scahsely recoup," said Wingo.

They dealt and played the hand, and the Governor strolled to the window.

"Three aces," Wingo announced, winning again handsomely. "I struck my luck too late," he commented to the on-lookers. While losing he had been able to sustain a smooth reticence; now he gave his thoughts freely to the company, and continually moved and fingered his increasing chips. The Governor was still looking out of the window, where he could see far up the street, when Wingo won the last hand, which was small. "That ends it, suh, I suppose?" he said to Hewley, letting the pack of cards linger in his grasp.

"I wouldn't let him off yet," said Ballard to Wingo from the window, with sudden joviality, and he came back to the players. "I'd make him throw five cold hands with me."

"Ah, Gove'nuh, that's yoh spo'tin' blood! Will you do it, Mistuh Hewley—a hun'red a hand?"

Mr. Hewley did it; and winning the first, he lost the second, third, and fourth in the space of an eager minute, while the Councillors drew their chairs close.

"Let me see," said Wingo, calculating, "if I lose this— why still—" He lost. "But I'll not have to ask you to accept my papuh, suh. Wingo liquidates. Fo'ty days at six dolluhs a day makes six times fo' is twenty-fo'—two hun'red an' fo'ty dolluhs spot cash in hand at noon, without computation of mileage to and from Silver City at fo' dolluhs every twenty miles, estimated according to the nearest usually travelled route." He was reciting part of the statute providing mileage for Idaho legislators. He had never served the public before, and he knew all the laws concerning compensation by heart. "You'll not have to wait fo' yoh money, suh," he concluded.

"Well, Mr. Wingo," said Governor Ballard, "it depends on yourself whether your pay comes to you or not." He spoke cheerily. "If you don't see things my way, our Treasurer will have to wait for his money." He had not expected to break the news just so, but it made as easy a beginning as any.

"See things yoh way, suh?"

"Yes. As it stands at present I cannot take the responsibility of paying you."

"The United States pays me, suh. My compensation is provided by act of Congress."

"I confess I am unable to discern your responsibility, Gove'nuh," said F. Jackson Gilet. "Mr. Wingo has faithfully attended the session, and is, like every gentleman present, legally entitled to his emoluments."

"You can all readily become entitled—"

"All? Am I—are my friends—included in this new depa'tyuh?"

"The difficulty applies generally, Mr. Gilet."

"Do I understand the Gove'nuh to insinuate—nay, gentlemen, do not rise! Be seated, I beg." For the Councillors had leaped to their feet.

"Whar's our money?" said Pete Cawthon. "Our money was put in thet yere box."

Ballard flushed angrily, but a knock at the door stopped him, and he merely said, "Come in."

A trooper, a corporal, stood at the entrance, and the disordered Council endeavored to look usual in a stranger's presence. They resumed their seats, but it was not easy to look usual on such short notice.

"Captain Paisley's compliments," said the soldier, mechanically, "and will Governor Ballard take supper with him this evening?"

"Thank Captain Paisley," said the Governor (his tone was quite usual), "and say that official business connected with the end of the session makes it imperative for me to be at the State-House. Imperative."

The trooper withdrew. He was a heavy-built, handsome fellow, with black mustache and black eyes that watched through two straight, narrow slits beneath straight black brows. His expression in the Council Chamber had been of the regulation military indifference, and as he went down the steps he irrelevantly sang an old English tune:

> *"Since first I saw your face I resolved*
> *To honor and re—*

"I guess," he interrupted himself as he unhitched his horse, "parrot and monkey hev broke loose."

The Legislature, always in its shirt-sleeves, the cards on the table, and the toddy on the floor, sat calm a moment, cooled by this brief pause from the first heat of its surprise, while the clatter of Corporal Jones's galloping shrank quickly into silence.

II

Captain Paisley walked slowly from the adjutant's office at Boisé Barracks to his quarters, and his orderly walked behind him. The captain carried a letter in his hand, and the orderly, though distant a respectful ten paces, could hear him swearing plain as day. When he reached his front door Mrs. Paisley met him.

"Jim," cried she, "two more chickens froze in the night." And the delighted orderly heard the captain so plainly that he had to blow his nose or burst.

The lady, merely remarking "My goodness, Jim," retired immediately to the kitchen, where she had a soldier cook baking, and feared he was not quite sober enough to do it alone. The captain had paid eighty dollars for forty hens this year at Boisé, and twenty-nine had now passed away, victims to the climate. His wise wife perceived his extreme language not to have been all on account of hens, however; but he never allowed her to share in his professional worries, so she stayed safe with the baking, and he sat in the front room with a cigar in his mouth.

Boisé was a two-company post without a major, and Paisley, being senior captain, was in command, an office to which he did not object. But his duties so far this month of May had not pleased him in the least. Theoretically, you can have at a two-company post the following responsible people: one major, two captains, four lieutenants, a doctor, and a chaplain. The major has been spoken of; it is almost needless to say that the chaplain was on leave, and had never been seen at Boisé by any of the present garrison; two of the lieutenants were also on leave, and two on surveying details—they had influence at Washington; the other captain was on a scout with General Crook somewhere near the Malheur Agency, and the doctor had only arrived this week. There had resulted a period when Captain Paisley was his own adjutant, quartermaster, and post surgeon, with not even an efficient sergeant to rely upon; and during this period his wife had stayed a good deal in the kitchen. Happily the doctor's coming had given relief to the hospital steward and several patients, and to the captain not only an equal, but an old friend, with whom to pour out his disgust; and together every evening they freely expressed their opinion of the War Department and its treatment of the Western army.

There were steps at the door, and Paisley hurried out. "Only you!" he exclaimed, with such frank vexation that the doctor laughed loudly. "Come in, man, come in," Paisley continued, leading him strongly by the arm, sitting him down, and giving him a cigar. "Here's a pretty how de do!"

"More Indians!" inquired Dr. Tuck.

"Bother! They're nothing. It's Senators—Councillors— whatever the Territorial devils call themselves."

"Gone on the war-path?" the doctor said, quite ignorant how nearly he had touched the Council.

"Precisely, man. War-path. Here's the Governor writing me they'll be scalping him in the State-House at twelve o'clock. It's past 11:30. They'll be whetting knives about now." And the captain roared.

"I know you haven't gone crazy," said the doctor, "but who has?"

"The lot of them. Ballard's a good man, and—what's his name?—the little Secretary. The balance are just mad dogs—mad dogs. Look here: 'Dear Captain'—that's Ballard to me. I just got it—'I find myself unexpectedly hampered this morning. The South shows signs of being too solid. Unless I am supported, my plan for bringing our Legislature to terms will have to be postponed. Hewley and I are more likely to be brought to terms ourselves—a bad precedent to establish in Idaho. Noon is the hour for drawing salaries. Ask me to supper as quick as you can, and act on my reply.' I've asked him," continued Paisley, "but I haven't told Mrs. Paisley to cook anything extra yet." The captain paused to roar again, shaking Tuck's shoulder for sympathy. Then he explained the situation in Idaho to the justly bewildered doctor. Ballard had confided many of his difficulties lately to Paisley.

"He means you're to send troops?" Tuck inquired.

"What else should the poor man mean?"

"Are you sure it's constitutional?"

"Hang constitutional! What do I know about their legal quibbles at Washington?"

"But, Paisley—"

"They're unsurrendered rebels, I tell you. Never signed a parole."

"But the general amnesty—"

"Bother general amnesty! Ballard represents the Federal government in this Territory, and Uncle Sam's army is here to protect the Federal government. If Ballard calls on the army it's our business to obey, and if there's any mistake in judgment it's Ballard's, not mine." Which was sound soldier common-sense, and happened to be equally good law. This is not always the case.

"You haven't got any force to send," said Tuck.

This was true. General Crook had taken with him both Captain Sinclair's infantry and the troop (or company, as cavalry was also then called) of the First.

"A detail of five or six with a reliable non-commissioned officer will do to remind them it's the United States they're bucking against," said Paisley. "There's a deal in the moral of these things. Crook—" Paisley broke off and ran to the door. "Hold his horse!" he called out to the orderly; for he had heard the hoofs, and was out of the house before Corporal Jones had fairly arrived. So Jones sprang off and hurried up, saluting. He delivered his message.

"Um—umpra—what's that? Is it *imperative* you mean?" suggested Paisley.

"Yes, sir," said Jones, reforming his pronunciation of that unaccustomed word. "He said it twiced."

"What were they doing?"

"Blamed if I—beg the captain's pardon—they looked like they was waitin' fer me to git out."

"Go on—go on. How many were there?"

"Seven, sir. There was Governor Ballard and Mr. Hewley and—well, them's all the names I know. But," Jones hastened on with eagerness, "I've saw them five other fellows before at a—at—" The corporal's voice failed, and he stood looking at the captain.

"Well? Where?"

"At a cock-fight, sir," murmured Jones, casting his eyes down.

A slight sound came from the room where Tuck was seated, listening, and Paisley's round gray eyes rolled once, then steadied themselves fiercely upon Jones.

"Did you notice anything further unusual, corporal?"

"No, sir, except they was excited in there. Looked like they might be goin' to hev considerable rough house—a fuss, I mean, sir. Two was in their socks. I counted four guns on a table."

"Take five men and go at once to the State-House. If the Governor needs assistance you will give it, but do nothing hasty. Stop trouble, and make none. You've got twenty minutes."

"Captain—if anybody needs arrestin'—"

"You must be judge of that." Paisley went into the house. There was no time for particulars.

"Snakes!" remarked Jones. He jumped on his horse and dashed down the slope to the men's quarters.

"Crook may be here any day or any hour," said Paisley, returning to the doctor. "With two companies in the background, I think Price's Left Wing will subside this morning."

"Supposing they don't?"

"I'll go myself; and when it gets to Washington that the commanding officer at Boisé personally interfered with the Legislature of Idaho, it'll shock 'em to that extent that the government will have to pay for a special commission of investigation and two tons of red tape. I've got to trust to that corporal's good sense. I haven't another man at the post."

Corporal Jones had three-quarters of a mile to go, and it was ten minutes before noon, so he started his five men at a run. His plan was to walk and look quiet as soon as he reached the town, and thus excite no curiosity. The citizens were accustomed to the sight of passing soldiers. Jones had thought out several things, and he was not going to order bayonets fixed until the final necessary moment. "Stop trouble and make none" was firm in his mind. He had not long been a corporal. It was still his first enlistment. His habits were by no means exemplary; and his frontier personality, strongly developed by six years of vagabonding before he enlisted, was scarcely yet disciplined into the military machine of the regulation pattern that it should and must become before he could be counted a model soldier. His captain had promoted him to steady him, if that could be, and to give his better qualities a chance. Since then he had never been drunk at the wrong time. Two years ago it would not have entered his free-lance heart to be reticent with any man, high or low, about any pleasure in which he saw fit to indulge; to-day he had been shy over confessing to the commanding officer his leaning to cock-fights—a sign of his approach to the correct mental attitude of the enlisted man. Being corporal had wakened in him a new instinct, and this State-House affair was the first chance he had had to show himself. He gave the order to proceed at a walk in such a tone that one of the troopers whispered to another, "Specimen ain't going to forget he's wearing a chevron."

III

The brief silence that Jones and his invitation to supper had caused among the Councillors was first broken by F. Jackson Gilet.

"Gentlemen," he said, "as President of the Council I rejoice in an interruption that has given pause to our haste and saved us from ill-considered expressions of opinion. The Gove'nuh has, I confess, surprised me. Befo' examining the legal aspect of our case I will ask the Gove'nuh if he is familiar with the sundry statutes applicable."

"I think so," Ballard replied, pleasantly.

"I had supposed," continued the President of the Council—"nay, I had congratulated myself that our weightiuh tasks of law-making and so fo'th were consummated yesterday, our thirty-ninth day, and that our friendly game of last night would be, as it were, the finis that crowned with pleashuh the work of a session memorable for its harmony."

This was not wholly accurate, but near enough. The Governor had vetoed several bills, but Price's Left Wing had had much more than the required two-thirds vote of both Houses to make these bills laws over the Governor's head. This may be called harmony in a manner. Gilet now went on to say that any doubts which the Governor entertained concerning the legality of his paying any salaries could easily be settled without entering upon discussion. Discussion at such a juncture could not but tend towards informality. The President of the Council could well remember most unfortunate discussions in Missouri between the years 1856 and 1860, in some of which he had had the honor to take part—*minima pars,* gentlemen! Here he digressed elegantly upon civil dissensions, and Ballard, listening to him and marking the slow, sure progress of the hour, told himself that never before had Gilet's oratory seemed more welcome or less lengthy. A plan had come to him, the orator next announced, a way out of the present dilemma, simple and regular in every aspect. Let some gentleman present now kindly draft a bill setting forth in its preamble the acts of Congress providing for the Legislature's compensation, and let this bill in conclusion provide that all members immediately receive the full amount due for their services. At noon both Houses would convene; they would push back the clock, and pass this bill before the term of their session should expire.

"Then, Gove'nuh," said Gilet, "you can amply vindicate yo'self by a veto, which, together with our votes on reconsideration of yoh objections, will be reco'ded in the journal of our proceedings, and copies transmitted to Washington within thirty days as required by law. Thus, suh, will you become absolved from all responsibility."

The orator's face, while he explained this simple and regular way out of the dilemma, beamed with acumen and statesmanship. Here they would make a law, and the Governor must obey the law!

Nothing could have been more to Ballard's mind as he calculated the fleeting minutes than this peaceful, pompous farce. "Draw your bill, gentlemen," he said. "I would not object if I could."

The Statutes of the United States were procured from among the pistols and opened at the proper page. Gascon Claiborne, upon another sheet of paper headed "Territory of Idaho, Council Chamber," set about formulating some phrases which began "Whereas," and Gratiot des Pères read aloud to him from the statutes. Ballard conversed apart with Hewley; in fact, there was much conversing aside.

"'Third March, 1863, c. 117, s. 8, v. 12, p. 811,'" dictated Des Pères.

"Skip the chaptuhs and sections," said Claiborne. "We only require the date."

"'Third March, 1863. The sessions of the Legislative Assemblies of the several Territories of the United States shall be limited to forty days' duration.'"

"Wise provision that," whispered Ballard. "No telling how long a poker game might last."

But Hewley could not take anything in this spirit. "Genuine business was not got through till yesterday," he said.

"'The members of each branch of the Legislature,'" read Des Pères, "'shall receive a compensation of six dollars per day during the sessions herein provided for, and they shall receive such mileage as now provided by law: *Provided,* That the President of the Council and the Speaker of the House of Representatives shall each receive a compensation of ten dollars a day.'"

At this the President of the Council waved a deprecatory hand to signify that it was a principle, not profit, for which he battled. They had completed their *Whereases,* incorporating the language of the several sections as to how the appropriation should be made, who disbursed such money, mileage, and, in short, all things pertinent to their bill, when Pete Cawthon made a suggestion.

"Ain't there anything 'bout how much the Gove'nuh gits?" he asks.

"And the Secretary?" added Wingo.

"Oh, you can leave us out," said Ballard.

"Pardon me, Gove'nuh," said Gilet. "You stated that yoh difficulty was not confined to Mr. Wingo or any individual gentleman, but was general. Does it not apply to yo'self, suh? Do you not need any bill?"

"Oh no," said Ballard, laughing. "I don't need any bill."

"And why not?" said Cawthon. "You've jist ez much earned yoh money ez us fellers."

"Quite as much," said Ballard. "But we're not alike—at present."

Gilet grew very stately. "Except certain differences in political opinions, suh, I am not awah of how we differ in merit as public servants of this Territory."

"The difference is of your own making, Mr. Gilet, and no bill you could frame would cure it or destroy my responsibility. You cannot make any law contrary to a law of the United States."

"Contrary to a law of the United States? And what, suh, has the United States to say about my pay I have earned in Idaho?"

"Mr. Gilet, there has been but one government in this country since April, 1865, and as friends you and I have often agreed to differ as to how many there were before then. That government has a law compelling people like you and me to go through a formality, which I have done, and you and your friends have refused to do each time it has been suggested to you. I have raised no point until now, having my reasons, which were mainly that it would make less trouble now for the Territory of which I have been appointed Governor. I am held accountable to the Secretary of the Treasury semiannually for the manner in which the appropriation has been expended. If you will kindly hand me that book—"

Gilet, more and more stately, handed Ballard the Statutes, which he had taken from Des Pères. The others were watching Ballard with gathering sullenness, as they had watched Hewley while he was winning Wingo's money, only now the sullenness was of a more decided complexion.

Ballard turned the pages. "'Second July, 1862. Every person elected or appointed to any office of honor or profit, either in the civil, military, or naval service,…shall, before entering upon the duties of such office, and before being entitled to any salary or other emoluments thereof, take and subscribe the following oath: I—'"

"What does this mean, suh?" said Gilet.

"It means there is no difference in our positions as to what preliminaries the law requires of us, no matter how we may vary in convictions. I as Governor have taken the oath of allegiance to the United States, and you as Councillor must do the same before you can get your pay. Look at the book."

"I decline, suh. I repudiate yoh proposition. There is a wide difference in our positions."

"What do you understand it to be, Mr. Gilet?" Ballard's temper was rising.

"If you have chosen to take an oath that did not go against yoh convictions—"

"Oh, Mr. Gilet!" said Ballard, smiling. "Look at the book." He would not risk losing his temper through further discussion. He would stick to the law as it lay open before them.

But the Northern smile sent Missouri logic to the winds. "In what are you superior to me, suh, that I cannot choose? Who are you that I and these gentlemen must take oaths befo' you?"

"Not before me. Look at the book."

"I'll look at no book, suh. Do you mean to tell me you have seen me day aftuh day and meditated this treacherous attempt?"

"There is no attempt and no treachery, Mr. Gilet. You could have taken the oath long ago, like other officials. You can take it to-day—or take the consequences."

"What? You threaten me, suh? Do I understand you to threaten me? Gentlemen of the Council, it seems Idaho will be less free than Missouri unless we look to it." The President of the Council had risen in his indignant oratorical might, and his more and more restless friends glared admiration at him. "When was the time that Price's Left Wing surrendered?" asked the orator. "Nevuh! Others have, be it said to their shame. We have not toiled these thousand miles fo' that! Others have crooked the pliant hinges of the knee that thrift might follow fawning. As fo' myself, two grandfathers who fought fo' our libuhties rest in the soil of Virginia, and two uncles who fought in the Revolution sleep in the land of the Dark and Bloody Ground. With such blood in my veins I will nevuh, nevuh, nevuh submit to Northern rule and dictation. I will risk all to be with the Southern people, and if defeated I can, with a patriot of old, exclaim,

> *More true joy an exile feels*
> *Than Caesuh with a Senate at his heels.*

Aye, gentlemen! And we will not be defeated! Our rights are here and are ours." He stretched his arm towards the Treasurer's strong-box, and his enthusiastic audience rose at the rhetoric. "Contain yo'selves, gentlemen," said the orator. "Twelve o'clock and our bill!"

"I've said my say," said Ballard, remaining seated.

"An' what'll ye do?" inquired Pete Cawthon from the agitated group.

"I forbid you to touch that!" shouted Ballard. He saw Wingo moving towards the box.

"Gentlemen, do not resort—" began Gilet.

But small, iron-gray Hewley snatched his pistol from the box, and sat down astraddle of it, guarding his charge. At this hostile movement the others precipitated themselves towards the table where lay their weapons, and Governor Ballard, whipping his own from his armhole, said, as he covered the table: "Go easy, gentlemen! Don't hurt our Treasurer!"

"Don't nobody hurt anybody," said Specimen Jones, opening the door.

This prudent corporal had been looking in at a window and hearing plainly for the past two minutes, and he had his men posted. Each member of the Council stopped as he stood, his pistol not quite yet attained; Ballard restored his own to its armhole and sat in his chair; little Hewley sat on his box; and F. Jackson Gilet towered haughtily, gazing at the intruding blue uniform of the United States.

"I'll hev to take you to the commanding officer," said Jones, briefly, to Hewley. "You and yer box."

"Oh, my stars and stripes, but that's a keen move!" rejoiced Ballard to himself. "He's arresting *us*."

In Jones's judgment, after he had taken in the situation, this had seemed the only possible way to stop trouble without making any, and therefore, even now, bayonets were not fixed. Best not ruffle Price's Left Wing just now, if you could avoid it. For a new corporal it was well thought and done. But it was high noon, the clock not pushed back, and punctual Representatives strolling innocently towards their expected pay. There must be no time for a gathering and possible reaction. "I'll hev to clear this State-House out," Jones decided. "We're makin' an arrest," he said, aloud, "and we want a little room." The outside bystanders stood back obediently, but the Councillors delayed. Their pistols were, with Ballard's and Hewley's, of course in custody. "Here," said Jones, restoring them. "Go home now. The commanding officer's waitin' fer the prisoner. Put yer boots on, sir, and leave," he added to Pete Cawthon, who still stood in his stockings. "I don't want to hev to disperse anybody more'n what I've done."

Disconcerted Price's Left Wing now saw file out between armed soldiers the Treasurer and his strong-box; and thus guarded they were brought to Boisé Barracks, whence they did not reappear. The Governor also went to the post.

After delivering Hewley and his treasure to the commanding officer, Jones with his five troopers went to the sutler's store and took a drink at Jones's expense. Then one of them asked the corporal to have another. But Jones refused. "If a man drinks much of that," said he (and the whiskey certainly was of a livid, unlikely flavor), "he's liable to go home and steal his own pants." He walked away to his quarters, and as he went they heard him thoughtfully humming his most inveterate song, "Ye shepherds tell me have you seen my Flora pass this way."

But poisonous whiskey was not the inner reason for his moderation. He felt very much like a responsible corporal to-day, and the troopers knew it. "Jones has done himself a good turn in this fuss," they said. "He'll be changing his chevron."

That afternoon the Legislature sat in the State-House and read to itself in the Statutes all about oaths. It is not believed that any of them sat up another night; sleeping on a problem is often much better. Next morning the commanding officer and Governor Ballard were called upon by F. Jackson Gilet and the Speaker of the House. Every one was civil and hearty as possible. Gilet pronounced the captain's whiskey "equal to any at the Southern, Saint Louey," and conversed for some time about the cold season, General Crook's remarkable astuteness in dealing with Indians, and other topics of public interest. "And concernin' yoh difficulty yesterday, Gove'nuh," said he, "I've been consulting the laws, suh, and I perceive yoh construction is entahley correct."

And so the Legislature signed that form of oath prescribed for participants in the late Rebellion, and Hewley did not have to wait for his poker money. He and Wingo played many subsequent games; for, as they all said in referring to the matter, "A little thing like that should nevuh stand between friends."

Thus was accomplished by Ballard, Paisley—and Jones—the Second Missouri Compromise, at Boisé City, Idaho, 1867—an eccentric moment in the eccentric years of our development westward, and historic also. That it has gone unrecorded until now is because of Ballard's modesty, Paisley's preference for the sword, and Jones's hatred of the pen. He was never known to write except, later, in the pages of his company roster and such unavoidable official places; for the troopers were prophetic. In not many months there was no longer a Corporal Jones, but a person widely known as Sergeant Jones of Company A; called also the "Singing Sergeant"; but still familiar to his intimate friends as "Specimen."

The Centennial Comment

ROBERT EDMOND ALTER

They propped the old man up in his bed where he could look into the room. It took four of them to do it: his grand-daughter, great-granddaughter, great-great-granddaughter, and Mr. Morris, the newspaperman from the North. It wasn't that he was heavy—he weighed less than a hundred—but he was brittle and a great deal of care had to be exerted when shifting him about.

He liked the upright position, liked to see what was going on. It hurt his back some, but he was used to that and he said nothing. He studied Lois, his great-great-grand-daughter, with his one good eye. She was seventeen and something to look at. She was a fool for tight sweaters, and with good reason; she stuck out like knobs on a smooth log. Fant liked that fine. Red fire, it didn't hurt any to look, did it? He grunted and reckoned not.

They all stopped talking and looked at him when they heard his sound. And that made him angry. *Bosh,* he thought, *now they're going to hang around and wait for me to speak.*

Like *a bunch of early birds looking at a worm,* Fant thought sourly. He ran his rheumy eye over Lois again and chuckled without sound. They didn't make 'em that way when he was that age. He remembered the girl by the turnpike on the march to Shiloh. She had been pretty enough, but you couldn't tell much about her figure from that Mother Hubbard her ma made her wear.

It had been a crazy march; the troops untrained, undisciplined, whooping and hollering through the woods, banging off their muskets...Beauregard had been so disgusted with them he'd damn near called off the attack. But the fellas could tell right off about that girl. She was the I-like-boys-like-crazy kind.

She stood beyond the split rail, bare-footed in the yard with the chickens scratching around her, hands on her hips, smiling at the troops, giving them a sort of under-and-around look. Why, she had them so excited they were ready to forget the war and let the Yanks have Tennessee.

It was young Hank Stanley—the boy who later became famous by presuming—who had talked Fant into it. "Go on. Slip in there and see if you can make off with a kiss. She's begging for it. There's not an officer in sight..." Hank had said.

Fant had been scared—he was just eighteen—but he didn't let on, couldn't, not with a couple hundred of his friends watching. He hopped the rail and approached the girl with a sort of salute.

"Mornin', Miss. I—them fellas there bet me I wouldn't take a kiss off you..."

"What did they bet?" she asked quick as a whip.

"Well—I dunno, a plug of tobacca or somethin', I guess."

She smiled, shy-like, and yet he knew it wasn't so. And she put her mouth up to his and kissed him hard. Didn't those fellas hoot and holler? By juckies, they nearly took the split rail apart.

"You win," she said coyly.

Fant was so embarrassed he didn't know what was happening. It wasn't until after he'd landed in the scrub weed and felt the pain in his backside, and turned to look at the big bewhiskered man standing over him, that he realized he was in trouble. It was the girl's pa, angrily vowing to kill him then and there. Fortunately Hank led a sortie against the old man and chased him and his daughter back into the house. But even so, Fant took an awful ribbing all the rest of the way to Shiloh, and he had to limp the first three miles.

Yes, it had been a pure-out circus. But the battle on April 6th, at Shiloh, changed all of that. It changed the thinking of every man in both armies, from the generals down to the drummer boys. The days of whooping and hollering and musket-banging on march was gone. War had become a grim business.

Old Fant looked at Mr. Morris. The newspaperman didn't want to hear about the girl and her pa by the turnpike. No, he wanted words of wisdom, a summing up of the great war that the present world could only read about. He didn't want facts. For a week now radio and TV had been feeding that to the public. Fant had even heard some of it himself, but it hadn't meant much to him. He'd been living with the facts of his life for one hundred and seventeen years.

One hundred years ago on this very day a group of South Carolina hotheads had fired the first shot on a square-block fort in the mouth of Charleston Harbour. The shot had marked the ending and the beginning of a new nation that had split in blood before it could understand the essential power of unity.

Fant had been seventeen. In March of the following year he had turned eighteen and had joined the Confederate forces, just before the battle of Shiloh. Now, on the day of the Centennial year, he was the only survivor of all those millions of boys who had gone off to the throb of drum and squeak of fife to fight for the blue and gray.

What could he say to this man who was waiting patiently to transmit his words to a curious public? The summing up was for historians of the time, not for the lone man who had been there. For that man it had been horror, boredom, fatigue, hate, mood...And how do you transmit a mood to people of the Twentieth Century?

That long-drawn, flat ridge of hill on the way to Antietam Creek, say. Thousands of men strung along the summit in double file, and with the curve of the hill you could look back as far as the eye could reach and see the tiny silhouettes—like ants walking on their hindlegs—pictured and moving against the vivid backdrop of turquoise sky. Dust and silence, punctuated by the gurgle of canteens, the clink and clank of equipment, the squeak and give of harness, the thud of thousands of boots. And then the sudden clear rise of Jimmy Noughton's Irish tenor, knifing into the dead air like a bugle call, singing of the minstrel boy who had gone to war.

And Fant had thought it the most glorious moment he'd ever known, had wished it could endure forever, because soldiering beat farming all hollow; soldiering was camaraderie, glory...And later in Bloody Lane, between Sharpsburg and Antietam Creek, he had cowered in terror under the whine and slam of shot, with dead men under his knees, with going-to-be dead men stumbling and coughing away from him, trying to say *God, God,* with cursing men rising over him to shoot and shout and...And how do you hand that to Mr. Morris of the Twentieth Century?

He sighed, wondering what to say to this man of another world. Should he tell him of the difference between a Yankee and a Secesh charge? That was fact. When the Yanks charged they shouted "Hurrah boys!" This encouraged them to go on but had no demoralizing effect on the enemy. But a Secesh charge went to the tune of the Rebel Yell, and this wailing scream struck terror into the hearts of the enemy; and whoever heard of a Reb needing encouragement to charge? Not that there was anything wrong with the Yanks when they finally got there; they would toe-the-mark like fighting demons, and you had to hammer 'em right down into the ground before their weaker sisters would call Uncle and run.

He thought fondly of the Rebel Yell, wishing he could hear it wailing discord once more, seeing in his mind the thousands of tanned, greasy necks stretching upward, the wet, dirty faces lifted to the sky, the whisker-rimmed mouths open, and the long reaching *Y-Yo-Yo—Wo-Wo-Wooo!* of the scream.

But he couldn't tell that to Mr. Morris from the North. Mr. Morris would smile politely, nod his head and say, "Very interesting, Mr. Austin. But can you give us a—uh—well a sort of summing up...You know, your interpretation of the Civil War from the viewpoint of a century later?"

A century later? He could tell of a boy he killed at Gettysburg...

The Yank had gotten twisted around in the confusion after Pickett's Bloody Angle had broken and had started to retreat with the Secesh troops instead of standing pat where he had belonged.

Young, scared half to death, too frightened to even lift his rifle and fight his way out, he had turned suddenly and faced Fant, screaming, "No! No, Reb! Don't shoot, damn you!" And Fant—not thinking, rattled—swung up his percussion carbine from the hip and blasted the Yank into a bloody somersault.

You don't forget something like that. You don't forget the boy's face, words, or even the new brass buttons on his tunic. You remember it even a century later. You wake up in the middle of a vast night in a damp bed and find yourself running and screaming with men who have been dead and forgotten for years, across furrowed and equipment-littered fields, and you hear again the blast and heave of the shells, and the whine of the minie balls, and you see the Yank before you, screaming and waving his hand, and you feel the tug of the trigger, the jar of the carbine going *ca-blam!* taste the powder...

And you sit bolt-up in bed and you cry into the dark room:

"I didn't know! Godamn it, I didn't know! How could I have known at that moment, at that place? I was frightened too, I tell you! I was callow and scared! I didn't think—couldn't." And then your wife or daughter, or granddaughter or great-granddaughter, came to you and mothered you back down into the damp sheets and told you it was all right, that you were only having a bad dream. But it wasn't a dream—it had been dying by living again.

But he couldn't tell that to Mr. Morris and to the people of Mr. Morris' world. Neither the North nor the South of today wanted to hear that the only surviving soldier of the Civil War had killed a Yankee boy that he could have taken prisoner, ninety-eight years ago...

He looked at the newspaperman again and frowned. *What is it you want to hear from me?* he asked himself. *What is it they all want to hear?* What would satisfy them? His granddaughter was showing Mr. Morris the Brady picture book of the war, pointing to the picture of the sunken road at Sharpsburg that Brady took right after the battle.

"This was the very spot that Grandfather fought at, Mr. Morris. Here in the centre—between those dead men and all that rubbish there."

Fant grimaced. He didn't know what part of Bloody Lane he had fought in. When he looked at the picture it all seemed the same to him—a ditch full of dead soldiers. Besides, Mr. Morris didn't give a hoot about where he fought; he wanted the summing up.

What would satisfy the man and send him on his way? Should he tell about Appomattox, about Lee's face at the end when he looked down at his men and said, "Men, we have fought through the war together. I have done my best for you. My heart is too full to say more." And how, with a final wave of his hat, he rode through the weeping army; and how they had followed him on foot, crying and slobbering in his wake; how Fant, overcome with emotion, had pushed his way frantically through his comrades to gain the general's side, and Lee's sad, fatherly face had turned down and he had murmured, "Let the boy through," and Fant had laid his hand on old Traveller's quivering flank and found that he was unable to say anything.

No, that wouldn't do. That meant nothing to the people of today. They hadn't been there, they hadn't seen him; they hadn't been a part of it—and he was the only part left.

Mr. Morris had set the book aside. He was smiling at Fant.

"Do you feel like talking now, Mr. Austin? Can you tell us anything? Your thoughts or emotions on the war? Just any comment for the Centennial?" he asked quietly.

Fant stared at the man from the North...And suddenly he smiled, because suddenly he knew that he had it—what they all wanted to hear, what would satisfy them when it was recorded.

None of them could see the smile; it was buried deep in the wrinkles of his face, lost in the folds of loose flesh. It was his secret laughing place. He opened his mouth and cleared his rusty throat and tried to fix a fierce aspect to his one good eye.

"Get the hell out of here, you damn Yankee," he commented huskily.